Dragon's Teeth

Cover image – reverse of The Queen's South Africa
Medal 1899 - 1902

© Nick McCarty

ISBN 978-0-9554771-4-0

Text prepared by www.willowebooks.org.uk

DRAGON'S TEETH

by

NICK McCARTY

KENELM 2012
London

About the author

Nick McCarty has been a professional writer for more than 40 years.

He has worked mostly for television on series like Bergerac, The Onedin Line, Z-Cars, Dangerfield, Spearhead and The Regiment which are being prepared for publication on Kindle.
He wrote the Anne Boleyn segment of The Six Wives of Henry VIII with Dorothy Tutin in the title rôle and Keith Michell as Henry.

He is an award-winning writer for radio. His original plays and adaptations include A Confidential Agent, A Tale of Two Cities, Hard Times, Zorba the Greek, Far from the Madding Crowd and many others

Previous publications

The Iliad Retold - with illustrations by Victor Ambrus (Kingfisher Books)
Troy, the story of its discovery by Heinrich Schliemann (Carlton Books)
Rome - a brief illustrated history (Carlton Books)
Alexander the Great (Carlton Books)
Fox - Cromwell's Spy
Fox - Assassin
Cats Tales
The Judas Gate

Contents

AMBUSH

1

The rock strewn hillside was tinder dry under the summer sun. The only vegetation was a few scrubby bushes and some brown patches of moss. Under the dust that served as earth was an outcrop of rock which shimmered in the heat. It was quite still.

In the valley a small river curved. It was mostly yellow mud, cracked and parched by months of clear blue skies. Still the water flowed, as it would flow for another six weeks or so. Then all that would be left of the Kaapshe River would be mud and a few stinking water-holes made foul by the men who used them.

Nothing moved across the arid valley. The track to the crossing point of the Kaapshe was made up of dust and sharp stones. Beside the track, the scrub was thin and there were huge boulders standing above the arid soil.

The eight men lay quite still. From the bare hillside they could look down on the river. The Wielver Commando waited and the sun burned them. For three hours now they had waited and the sight of the flowing water below was torture.

Jan Meyer looked across the hillside and smiled. These men were his men, his commando. He had trained them; he led them and they knew and trusted him even though he was younger than most.

The commando had nothing but their guns and their bullets and their hardy ponies, but they harassed and they killed and the whole British Empire could go hang for them.

Jan spat. His riding boots, which were new, hurt him

at the ankle. He would be forced to slit them again. Whenever he made them, he always forgot and had to slit the leather with his knife after a few days in the saddle.

Jan was lying behind a boulder looking down the valley. Carefully he took off his broad-brimmed hat. He wiped the sweat from the inside rim and looked at this dusty shapeless thing that his wife had once given to him, new, from the town. She was in the town each year from the farm. But never now. So, no new hats, no new anything except what they could make. Jan replaced his hat and grimaced at the ache in his ankle.

'At least we Boers can make most things we need,' he thought.

He looked across at Piet Leyds and smiled at the boy. He was nervous. It was his first time with the commando and perhaps he was too young. Thirteen years old and eager to come. Jan hadn't wanted to take him. His mother didn't want him to come.

The boy nodded and smiled across the gap to Jan. His mouth a thin, nervous line and his eyes strained. It was a long time to wait in the heat without shade.

Jan knew that the convoy would come and when it came there would be a field-gun and ammunition. He thought of the things he could do with that gun. The trains he could blow up, the bridges he could destroy, the columns he could surprise. He looked again at the boy and began to worry.

If anything went wrong, if anything betrayed their position before the right time, then they were done for. It was an exposed situation they were in and they had their ponies hidden over the rim of the hills. To cross the ground, with little cover, would make them sitting ducks for good marksmen. The boy might break, he might shoot too soon.

Jan cursed his soft heart for bringing the lad. He

2

eased the bandoleer of bullets from under his chest, checked his rifle again and screwed up his eyes to look down the valley and across the water of the river.

Nothing moved. The eight men watched.

Piet ran his tongue over his dry, cracked lips and thought for a moment about his mother whom he had left alone in the veldt. His father had joined a commando and had died. He was buried somewhere between this river and the mountains further up country. Piet was frightened by the knot in his stomach. His father's rifle lay against his cheek. He waited for the word and knew that Jan must be pleased with him or he would be sent back to the farm.

Jan lay so still he hardly seemed to breathe, his beard roughly trimmed and his hair hanging below the broad, broken hat he always wore. He had eyes that seemed black when he was angry and that seldom smiled, even when his mouth did. Piet was more afraid of Jan than of what would come next; the shooting, the bullets.

Across the valley a bird rose from its rocky nest beside the river. Jan looked up and saw the solitary horseman, a scout, riding forward. Jan had been thinking for a moment about his wife and the farm he had carved with her from the veldt. All of them were farmers, and each Boer farm gave something, or someone, to the fight.

They were lucky with their women, Jan thought, as he sucked the pebble in his mouth. Their women now looked after the farms, for the men could not be there.

Poor Truus, who had only the one child. A boy, at least, he was. No matter how they tried, they were unable to get more. Truus prayed, he knew, and read the bible that was his father's and his father's before, but God had decided that she should have no more. So little Piet would have the farm one day. And it would be green and running with cattle and water because Jan had promised his woman it would be. She had smiled at him and patted her belly and he had sworn on her belly that it would have all he could find. And Truus smiled softly at him and he was made a man by her.

Anders raised his rifle, an easy shot, no more than three hundred yards, but Anders was too old a hand to shoot the scout. They wanted the convoy. They wanted the field-gun. That was important. That and the ammunition. Anders lowered his gun and the scout rode on. He saw nothing move on the hillside above the crossing.

Jan looked across at the boy and winked at Piet and, tapping his rifle, he shook his head. The boy understood and grinned.

One of the commando groaned when the scout stopped at the water, dismounted and took a drink. The horse also drank a little. Slowly the scout straightened up and looked about him. The rim of the hills was beginning to purple as the sun dipped lower in the sky. Shadows were forming over the valley, but the heat was still there in the rock and even now was beginning to beat back off the ground where they lay.

Jan opened and closed the fingers of his right hand and tried to move his right leg. One pebble struck against another and Jan froze. His ankle could go on hurting, he dared not move again until the time came.

The scout remounted and swung the horse back along the track. He would be joining the convoy, reporting what he had seen. Jan smiled. It would not be long now. He sensed the other men preparing themselves for the moment when the convoy would appear round the bluff beyond the river crossing. The scout was already out of sight. Only dust marked his passage.

As the convoy approached the water, Jan knew that the mules would become agitated. They hadn't drunk properly for a day and a half at least. The smell of the water would set them on edge, like cows with a stud bull. The mules would quicken their pace, the soldiers too would pick up speed and soon they would be doubling for the water. The scout would have reported all clear and these gentlemen in khaki would be anxious to fill canteens, to drink, even to wash. As the first animal began to drink, that was the time.

The eight men lay and watched the shadows inching towards them across the rocks. The men were silent, and even Piet held his breath and watched and waited and wondered if he had a bullet in the breech. He dared not check now. Too late for that. A slow bead of sweat ran across his eyes and he blinked it away.

Distinctly across the silent valley the Wielver Commando heard the rattle of harness and the groaning of wagon wheels over the rough track.

2

A mile and a half from the river crossing, a string of mules hauled a field-gun, boxes of ammunition and stores. D Company of the Cotswolds were over two hundred miles up country from HQ and they needed the field-gun urgently. The convoy had been pushed hard across the burning veldt and the men were beginning to show signs of anger. An irritability caused not by the work, but by the heat, the dust, the flies and the bad track they were following.

They were as good a group of soldiers as drew breath when it came to fighting, but this business of hauling a mule train across the country was not to their liking.

A platoon of men, a lieutenant and a dozen mules is an unwieldy party to march anywhere, and when they are bogged down with a field-gun and its limber, they are almost impossible to move. Lieutenant Willoughby had done it, though. Two more days' march at this pace should see them at D Company HQ.

James Willoughby wiped the sweat from his face and cursed his luck. For six days he had been moving them on at first light and bedding them down in the dark, and it was a strain. The men were thirsty and irritable and who could blame them? Wasn't he irritable himself?

James Willoughby was angered by the attacks the Boers were making on the Army. No one would stand and fight. He supposed no one could be blamed for that. After all, the small Boer rebel groups would have to face the might of the British Empire if they stood and fought it out. They hadn't the stomach for it. It was a slow business, war. Slower even than these mules.

Willoughby moved his horse forward alongside the gun and nodded at the sergeant.

'Another half an hour, Sergeant. Then we'll take an

hour's rest. There will be water, a river.'

The Sergeant nodded at the young officer. He turned to the men marching with the gun.

'You heard the Lieutenant — thirty minutes and you'll be rolling in the waters of Heaven, you lucky bleeders.'

Not one of the men smiled and Willoughby noted it. They'd stopped singing after the second day and now the smiles had gone. The sooner they reached D Company the better for them all.

For six days now, James Willoughby had marched and ridden the veldt, holding the column together, guiding it, navigating for it, along the track that was hardly marked on the ground and was certainly on no map. Beyond that bluff ahead was the river, he knew that for certain. An hour to wash and to clean the horses and to drink would put them all in a better humour. He turned in the saddle and looked along the column of marching men. As he looked, he saw at the end another figure on a horse. For six days now he had been saddled with Saunders. Captain Saunders who watched him and the way he handled the convoy and said little. Captain Saunders, whom he disliked, and who, he was certain, disliked him as heartily.

The commanding officer had smiled when he announced the news just an hour before the convoy outspanned.

'Oh, by the way James, you'll be taking Captain Saunders. He'll be joining your convoy. He's seconded to D Company for a month.'

Perhaps the only reason for anyone to laugh was that Alfred Slingsby was going to have to suffer Saunders for a month at D Company. Willoughby had looked at Major Hallam when he told him the news and he had whistled.

'Well, James? What's that for?'

Willoughby had shrugged. It was none of his business. He'd taken the instructions and dispatches for Captain Slingsby and saluted, before turning smartly out of the Cotswold office. His boots had thumped on the wooden verandah like a funeral roll. He would give his teeth not to have to ride with Saunders for six days or more. Six days to put up with superior airs and graces. It was going to be hard enough to get the men and the mules and the gun, intact, across the veldt without the complication of having Dorothy's husband riding with him.

The convoy was ready. The mules were still, save for the twitching of their ears against the flies. The men ready to march two hundred miles across the veldt, Sergeant Rowan standing in the dust of the small parade square before the regimental office. Willoughby had mounted his horse slowly and looked across the square for a sign of Saunders, and eventually he had arrived. He rode up to Willoughby who sat on his horse and waited.

'Sorry, old man. Didn't mean to keep you,' he'd said and Willoughby had nodded.

'Do carry on, James. Look, it is your show.'

Captain Saunders smiled a little at the lieutenant. Willoughby rode across the square to the sergeant who snapped a salute to him. Willoughby saluted him gravely.

'Captain Saunders will ride with us, Sergeant.'

'Yes sir, certainly sir.'

Sergeant Rowan knew the situation as well as any man in the Regiment. Willoughby's business enterprises in South Africa had not paid off. He hadn't two pennies to rub together and was senior lieutenant. Saunders, a newly made-up captain with oodles of the stuff — you only had to look at their horses to see. Sergeant Rowan hesitated. Saunders was still a distance off.

'You will take your orders, Sergeant, from me.'

Willoughby allowed an edge to creep into his voice. The sergeant was surprised — pleased in a way. It made things easier to know where you stood.

'Very good sir.'

Willoughby watched Saunders as he sat upright on his horse. Saunders had sent for his own stable when he had seen the squalid little mounts sent out from Australia for the use of the British Army.

'It must be nice to have the money,' Willoughby thought bitterly. He had his pay and a hundred and fifty or so a year. It hardly covered the cost of his uniforms. Why Saunders hadn't joined a fashionable regiment Willoughby had no notion. And to be constantly reminded of Dorothy — day in and day out under this heat. Six days driving the men, six days of the dust and heat, six days of remembering an autumn afternoon at Richard Gaunt's home in Gloucestershire. It wasn't easy to forget, even in South Africa. Even in a war.

The convoy struggled on for two days and nights. Sergeant Rowan seemed happy enough when they bivouacked for the night. The men had begun to grumble after the second day. Willoughby was pushing them hard. Even Saunders had remarked upon it.

'It's a cruel pace you set, Lieutenant Willoughby, don't you think?' Saunders had asked.

They were sitting with their backs to the stone walls of a sheep kraal. The pickets were out and the Sergeant was cleaning his rifle nearby. Most of the men lay sleeping on the ground.

Willoughby looked across at Saunders and didn't answer for a moment.

'D'you think so, Captain? The gun is needed. The ammunition is also needed. And the Boer would love it. When they get wind, they'll be on us, will they not?'

Saunders had shrugged and Willoughby lost his temper.

'You wouldn't know, of course. Spent too much time at HQ and not enough in the field.'

He regretted the outburst as soon as he'd uttered it. But already it was too late and he could not bring himself to apologize. Captain Saunders had merely looked at him and smiled and turned away to sleep.

'Goodnight James,' he'd said and Willoughby could have killed the man. He looked up to find Sergeant Rowan standing beside him.

'Check the pickets, sir?' he'd asked and, glad of an excuse, Willoughby had agreed and gone with the older man.

Beyond the kraal walls, the veldt was velvet black. Slowly the two men approached the first picket.

'All quiet, sir,' the man had reported and they had moved on slowly.

After the pickets had been checked, the sergeant had stopped a moment on the far side of the kraal from the captain. He knew that Lieutenant Willoughby was under considerable strain.

'It's all right sir, you know that. We'll get that gun past the Boojers, no trouble.'

'It's our job, Sergeant,' James replied shortly. The sergeant smiled.

'Yes sir, it's our job. You'll get it to D Company, sir. You'll see.'

'And you'll keep a civil tongue, Sergeant, or I'll know the reason why.' Willoughby looked at the sergeant, who stared at him for a moment and then looked away.

'Yes sir. Sorry.'

It wasn't anything at all, but somehow the march had gone sour from then on. A routine but hard convoy had turned sick on him and Willoughby laid the blame squarely on Captain Rupert Saunders.

Dorothy Saunders was out here now, nursing in the

Officers' Hospital with Mrs Gaunt. Willoughby hadn't dared to see her when he was in Pretoria. God knows he had wanted to. He had worked hard to forget her, but had not succeeded. He had driven himself and his men hard over the veldt, because of her husband who watched and smiled and said so little. 'Your show, old man,' and that settled that. Willoughby was in charge. With luck, two days should see them at D Company and Saunders would be out of his hair. Willoughby turned and looked at the trudging red-faced men behind him. Still not a smile at the thought of the river ahead. The dust puffed up each time the men laid a foot to the warm ground. The men at the rear of the platoon had to be brought forward in the line of march every so often, to free them from the clogging dust that rose up over the column.

In England the summer of 1900 was ending, and people assumed the Boer War to be virtually over. People had celebrated the relief of Mafeking as if the troops would be home, victorious, within weeks. Pretoria was taken and Lord Roberts had ridden into the town like a Roman General. The Boer army had surrendered and President Kruger was somewhere in Europe. In London the war was almost forgotten. Wounded soldiers, who had at first excited sympathy and compassion, now only raised mild interest.

'The war's over, bar the shouting, dammit,' was the common cry. In South Africa the soldiers knew better.

As the summer faded into autumn, and Hampshire lanes were turning yellow and fiery red, the veldt of Africa dried out slowly and the summer came south. And with the heat of the summer came a different kind of fighting, a new kind of war — guerrilla war.

Willoughby turned in his saddle to watch the men stumble by. Bristol was never so hot; the West Country was never like this. Willoughby watched the line of khaki pass him, and heard the mule drivers' curses.

These were soldiers of the Queen.

Suddenly from the right, behind the bluff, a solitary horseman raced towards the column. One of the forward pickets reined in beside him, in a flurry of dust

'Well, Jackson?'

'Nothing sir. All quiet ahead. The river's low, sir.'

'Water, though?' Willoughby asked anxiously.

'Yes, sir. Enough. And not spoiled, sir.'

Willoughby nodded and noted the caked saliva and dust down the flanks of the horse.

'Very well, Jackson. And go easier with that horse. It'll not take too kindly to hard riding. Not in this heat.'

The private saluted and rode back into the line. Already another scout was taking his place forward of the line of march. It would be a poor time for the column to be ambushed.

Willoughby urged his horse forward alongside Saunders.

3

Pretoria was still, beneath the afternoon sunshine. Few people moved under the awnings down Church Street East. Harvey Greenacre at The Corner was closed, so no one could buy bedsteads or glass. Across the rough road, Cuthbert's Boot Store, a more imposing building, was also closed for trade. Two or three buildings down the street were shored up. The result of the struggles to take the town perhaps. But since Lord Roberts of Khandahar had ridden into the town in June, the place had been quiet.

Across Church Square, Dorothy could see a wagon being hauled by five teams of oxen. The wagon-master was cracking his hide whip and shouting in Afrikaans. Two farmers jogged slowly across the dusty square towards the domes of the civic buildings. They passed the carpet store near the Gothic church and were hidden by a clump of trees that shaded a small part of the area.

Outside the civic building, some soldiers stood. There was no shade on this side of the square, and only inside the buildings was there a promise of cool dimness.

Dorothy looked at the quiet scene from her hotel window across the square. She smiled a little at the incongruousness of the main building that looked like a cross between a Roman Temple and the buildings in the City of London. And beside it, another place equally odd, with three tiers of balconies like some vast theatre. But there was no show to look at. Not here. Not in Pretoria, now. More soldiers loitered in the dust at the end of the road. There would be four or five officers in the reception area of the hotel, beside the potted plants. And from the green baize room that housed the billiard table would come the dull click of the balls. A muted murmur of sound only from the players. The town was asleep in the afternoon sunshine.

Dorothy turned from the window. Her room was cool, and for that she was thankful. The huge bed, the imposing wardrobes and wash-stand filled the room. After three weeks on the boat Dorothy had felt cramped, but she had promised herself space when she arrived in Africa. And here she was, cooped up in an hotel room, unable to turn round — or held in the round of hospital, social evening, sleeping, like some beetle trapped in a box. She was exhausted by it. She felt tired at the thought of the hospital, but she had a duty to do and there was no way to escape it. She sighed and ran her finger across the glass of the mirror on the dressing-table. Outside, she could hear the man cursing his oxen. At least she felt he must be cursing, though his language was such a harsh thing that it was hard to tell if he was shouting endearments. She smiled, she doubted it. They were a dour people these Boers and sullen, now that their town was taken. It was such a futile gesture they were making, to try to hold off the British Army. It was only a matter of time. It was all only a matter of time. She thought of Rupert again and heard the whip on the backs of the oxen.

She had told herself a thousand times that she didn't really wish her husband any harm. She had lain awake at nights after he had gone with the convoy. The irony was that she had never spoken properly with James Willoughby since that day, over a year ago, when they had promised never to see each other again. And now Rupert, her husband, was riding with him. What a waste the grand gesture was. The sacrifice for others was only a sacrifice of herself.

James Willoughby had the Army, he had this war. And Dorothy almost regretted that she had no part in it, other than her duties in the hospital.

She had heard how the Boer women helped their

14

men, how their farms were used as centres for the Boer troops to recover from wounds, to rest and to hide from British patrols. Many of the Boer women, apparently, could shoot like their men or better, could look after the farms and their children while the men were away on the veldt. Such a lonely life. Dorothy shuddered at the thought. To be alone in one of those squalid little huts, miles from the nearest white person. Not knowing if the next visitors were to be a commando or a British patrol or a native raiding party.

Dorothy sighed and picked up the small photograph of Rupert that he had given to her on his last evening. The photographer had caught his likeness in the stiff pose. The dress uniform of the Cotswolds festooned with braid, the cap at the correct angle, the face calm and severe. He didn't smile often and never with his eyes. Usually, indeed, his smiles were at the expense of someone else. She put the picture down. After all, it only reminded her more severely of James. Dorothy stared at her reflection. Poor Rupert. Didn't he have his war as well and his property and investments here to think of? What had she gained from giving up her man? Respect-ability of course, acceptance into the best society, dull society, her husband's friends. But what a sadness was left. She had seen James Willoughby only once since that day when the Regiment had left England for the war, and that was here, in Pretoria.

Church Street stretched out into the country beyond the town and she had been standing looking at some flowers when he had ridden past. He'd looked in her direction and ridden on. It was as well, she supposed at the time, for if Rupert should hear that they had met on this quiet road, he would have been angry, jealous perhaps. James would not dare break down the barrier they had put up. It would always be up to her.

It seemed so futile, so wasteful when, at any minute,

she might find herself nursing either of them; her husband or James. Maimed, without an arm, a leg, an eye, or any of the other disgusting rewards of war. She kicked off her slippers and lay back on the cool sheets.

Dorothy Saunders, long-haired beauty, wife of a captain in the Cotswolds — a man of acumen, a collector of considerable talent. Land, houses, pictures, even businesses, he collected with faultless skill. His wife, all agreed, was a brilliant addition to the collection. Some did find her reserved, rather distant, and put it down to shyness. Others found her arrogant. But they all found her beautiful.

Dorothy smiled at the thought. If they could only see her in the Officers' Hospital, ministering to those men. Then the society gossips would have their noses put out of joint. She had never worked so hard in her life. Her hands ached and her back was on fire. Lifting and carrying, holding and comforting men who might have been her brothers, her husband, her lovers — she sighed and turned her pale face to the wall and ached to cry, but the tears were already gone.

Outside, as the sun began to dip, the square was springing to life again. The shadows from the tall trees lay over the sandy square and pointed at the church. Two old ladies walked towards the green carpet store. A mule brayed and, far in the distance, Dorothy could hear the crash of rifles. The men were practising on the range again.

Along Church Street the shops began to open. Mackay Brothers would soon be trading, and people could move in the cool shadows as the heat abated. Downstairs the hotel pianola was playing softly, and the blacks who sat on the steps at the back of the hotel would be humming the tune, perhaps. Dorothy wondered what they thought of the war — a white man's war.

Someone passed her room. Dorothy heard a door

16

slam further up the corridor, they didn't return.

By now, James and her husband, the convoy, the gun, the ammunition to make more shattered men, would be well on its way to D Company HQ.

Dorothy smiled as she thought of Richard Gaunt and Captain Slingsby, waiting up there for the supplies and for the letters that must be rare enough for a soldier. They were so very far away and she supposed that, for the men, a letter was a rare occurrence indeed. It was even worse for those with wives who didn't know how to write. For a year now, they had been here and would know nothing of their families. 'It was a pitiful existence for a man,' she thought.

It would be easier for Mrs Gaunt to understand than for Dorothy. Wasn't she wife of the Colonel of the Regiment? She was the daughter of a soldier. For Dorothy it was a strange world, distant. Oh, she had known something of what she was marrying into. Even though her father had seemed concerned for her, he had married them in his church and blessed the marriage. She could feel the tears behind her eyes. The marriage was bitterness and ashes in her mouth now. It was a place in society she was marrying, not an army and a war. A bitter war like this.

Dorothy sighed and rolled over, creasing her dress. She lay staring at the ceiling, her pale grey eyes quite calm suddenly. She knew what she must do, what she would do if she had her opportunity again. She smiled at the thought and sat up. She looked at her self in the mirror and grimaced at the sight.

Five wasted years. She looked for the creases of age at the eyes and along her throat and found smooth, pale skin. Only a wary light behind her eyes showed how she had suffered over the years. Suffered mostly from the boredom and uselessness of her marriage. Someone knocked on the door.

'Come in,' Dorothy called and the door opened and closed gently.

Dorothy didn't turn from the mirror. She could see Mrs Gaunt standing watching her from the door. The pearly grey of her uniform with the white, starched collar was a strange contrast to the superb diamond cluster she wore on her breast. A present from her husband who had died. Some said of a broken heart. Rupert said it was 'merely old age'.

Mrs Gaunt waited for Dorothy to turn round. She knew that Dorothy was unhappy. It seemed such a shame that the gladness had gone out of her. But woman has a duty, and marriage is irrevocable. Vows taken are to be kept. Mrs Gaunt, however, felt a strong compassion for the girl before her, knowing that her marriage was unhappy.

Dorothy turned from the mirror and looked at her.

'We're going to the hospital, Dorothy.'

Dorothy flushed under her steady regard and was sure that Mrs Gaunt could read her mind. She lowered her eyes and waited.

'You're all right, my dear?' Mrs Gaunt quietly took her arm and stood for a moment by her. Dorothy nodded and took up the hairbrush. She began to drag it through her hair.

I'll only be a moment.'

Dorothy looked at Mrs Gaunt.

'Well?' she asked and Mrs Gaunt shook her head. 'I'm perfectly all right, Mrs Gaunt. Truly.' She insisted.

'You're looking rather tired, my dear. That's all.' Mrs Gaunt smiled. 'Are you sure you feel able to come this afternoon?'

Dorothy shrugged. 'I have to. Don't I? I'd only be a burden if I stayed here. There's work to do.'

Mrs Gaunt looked around the room helplessly, as if she had no wish to say any more.

18

'Don't I?'

The older woman looked back at Dorothy and shook her head. She said, 'I didn't tell you, I saw Lieutenant Willoughby when he was here. He said he might call on you. Did he?'

Dorothy's answer stuck in her throat. She shook her head.

'I see. I thought he might pay his respects. It was rather rude of him, don't you think, Dorothy?'

Dorothy shook her head. Did Mrs Gaunt know? Was she testing the ground? Checking, perhaps.

'No. No, he didn't come. I — I don't think he and Rupert see eye to eye — it's a pity.'

Mrs Gaunt moved across the room to the window. She looked out. Dorothy stood with her cape in her hands, waiting to go. Mrs Gaunt sighed and turned back into the room.

'Be careful, my dear. Please take care.'

Outside, a man was still cursing his team of oxen. Dorothy heard his whip crash on to their straining backs.

Dorothy's head was whirling. The heat, the dust. She sat down.

'You're not well, Dorothy. Sit still.' Mrs Gaunt poured some tepid water from the water jug on the wash-stand and Dorothy drank slowly, gaining time.

'We like James, of course. But he is not your husband.'

Dorothy shook her head. All their attempts to hide it, their efforts to stay apart, to excite no gossip — and Mrs Gaunt had known it from the beginning.

Dorothy looked up at Mrs Gaunt. 'You're very kind.' She tried to smile past the tight lips that held back her grief.

'He is not your husband?' Mrs Gaunt repeated. Dorothy shook her head.

'No, he is not my husband.'

19

'Richard likes him, respects him very much.'

'I know,' said Dorothy. 'I know he does.'

'And you had best be careful Dorothy. I'm sorry, I didn't mean to pry. I didn't even want to mention it.'

Mrs Gaunt was upset by her indiscretion. Dorothy took her hand.

'We haven't met. Not properly. Not for years. Not since we were your house-guests that autumn. We tried to marry Charlotte off to James and really I . . . , I . . .' Dorothy pushed her hair out of her eyes and looked up at Mrs Gaunt. She was cooler now, more reserved than Dorothy had ever known her.

'We promised we would never see each other — it's such a waste.'

Dorothy knew very well that Mrs Gaunt had loved her husband and that the Colonel had loved her. While, for Rupert, she was a convenience, a face to take to regimental dinners and social shows. She was necessary to his style of life, but not in any way to him. Mrs Gaunt had a rigid code that she followed, and that had brought her happiness and love. For any friend of hers, or of her daughter's, to break that code was unthinkable. Dorothy had been set to plough a furrow and plough it she must, to the end.

Dorothy put down the cape and her bag and sat on the edge of the bed, staring at the wall. She was quite still.

'We shall go across to the hospital now, Dorothy. Perhaps you'll take a carriage and follow us later.'

Mrs Gaunt left and closed the door quietly behind her. Dorothy sat looking into the mirror. She felt so wasted. So desolate.

4

Richard looked at the burning sky. It was weeks since they had seen rain. Across the veldt, from D Company HQ, the heat shimmered off the rock and sand. Even to the south, and towards the mountains, where it had been green grazing only six weeks ago, the earth was scorched by the blaze of the sun.

Though now the sun was dipping away and the shadows of the buildings lay darkly on the beaten earth square outside the company office, Richard was still aware of his shirt sticking to his back and aware of the dust and dirt blown into every crevice of his clothes. His sola topee lay on the table on the veranda outside his room. Richard flicked at the dust with a swagger-stick his mother had given him before he left for the war. It had been his father's and she thought it might bring him luck. Richard smiled to himself and looked at the slim length of polished wood. His mother was amusing sometimes and she'd borne her loss, when his father died, better than most had expected.

Richard turned as Captain Slingsby walked out on to the veranda.

'Well, Richard, any sign?' Slingsby asked. Richard shook his head and strolled towards the steps.

'Nothing,' he said, and Slingsby sat in a wicker chair by the table and took out his handkerchief to wipe his hands, which were sticky with sweat. Writing reports always made him sweat. Slingsby grinned ruefully. Not his game, this writing and requisitioning. All took up too much time and left too little for soldiering.

'Pickets all quiet?' He knew Richard had checked only twenty minutes ago, but he seemed to feel it necessary, always, to double-check. Richard was beginning to realize that Slingsby wasn't as sure of himself as he appeared.

'All quiet. Yes. No sight nor sound of the Boer. Nor likely to be,' he said.

He was bored with the lack of activity. They'd been here now for two months and hadn't moved other than to make routine patrols. They'd seen nothing of Boer commandos, and even when they had intelligence that a commando was hiding up in one of the farms across the veldt, they never arrived in time. The men were restive.

They'll wait till they get orders,' said Slingsby.

'They'll die of boredom damn soon. You know that.'

Slingsby shook his head. 'We shall all die of it, Richard. Shan't we?'

Across the square, Sullivan and Sergeant Holly stood in the shade outside the stables. They knew that the convoy was expected either tomorrow or the day after.

So far, they'd been occupied in skirmishing patrols and seen nothing. With the big gun it might be a different matter.

Sergeant Holly spat in the dust at his feet and looked back into the stables. Three horses were being groomed. They shone in the dim light of the stalls, but within an hour of being out, they'd be caked with dust and fit only for the knacker's yard. It was the pig's ear of a job this, sitting for weeks with nothing at all happening.

'It's no bloody soldier's life this, Sergeant.'

Sullivan didn't look at the sergeant when he spoke. Holly looked at the tall Irishman. Sullivan just leaned back against the wooden walls and looked over the square at the two officers sitting on their veranda.

'It's what we're ordered to do, Sullivan. That's all.'

Sullivan grunted and smoothed his hard hands over the front of his khaki trousers. He'd the smell of horses on them and all about him, and he hated the beasts. Wasn't that why he'd been broken from corporal when he had come out here? He'd let a man go who had the evil nature of some of these four-legged beasts they were currying in that bloody stable.

He'd let a man go who was too much of a coward to face the life they had out here. Sullivan was sick in his gut at the thought. Hadn't they reduced him to the ranks and got his family out of the married quarters they'd had? For private soldiers only had women, not wives, and no army was responsible for the women. His wife was forced to a squalor in Cheltenham such as he had never wished on her. He cursed the day he had joined the Army, and also the names of the officers who had reduced him to the ranks again. He looked across the square and he almost heaved with the anger in him. And that bastard, Captain Slingsby, had smiled as he told him the sentence.

'Serve you right Sullivan. Make you damn well sit up and take notice.'

Holly knew what the soldier was thinking and that Sullivan could cause trouble. Too much time for brooding and he'd start to talk and he'd the silver tongue on him all right. Hadn't Holly heard him in the non-coms' mess back in England?

'Easy Sullivan, easy.'

Sullivan looked at the sergeant and smiled a tight smile.

'I'm thinking a little about Meg, Sergeant. She's a terrible time of it at Cheltenham, and no help from the Regiment at all. Was it her fault I was broken? Was it her fault that big — that thing got away at all? It was not. And her suffering.'

'Easy man, easy. They'll make you up again soon enough.'

And Sergeant Holly knew he was lying, for he knew that the Captain didn't like the tall Irishman, any more than the Irishman liked Slingsby.

Holly sighed. He'd the peace to keep and it wasn't

23

easy. The men were bored with days of nothing to do except look at the flat country and the fiery heat burning off it like vapour.

The sun sank lower and the ordinary life of the company began again. A group of men were doing fatigues and doubled passed the company office; another platoon were taken off for rifle practice. The horses were led out for exercise. The little square began to take life.

Richard Gaunt watched it and wondered how the estate was managing without him. His mother had tried to keep it up, but it was work for a man. Richard smiled ruefully and watched the pathetic string of horses as they passed him. Across the square he saw Sullivan watching him again. He wondered what was the matter with the man. He seemed surly, bitter — surely he wasn't still angered by his breaking.

Richard got up from the table and walked across the square, slapping the swagger-stick on his thigh.

The Headquarters of D Company was listless. Waiting for the supplies, wailing for the gun, waiting for the convoy to arrive with dispatches, letters — waiting.

The heat-bemused flies began to crawl from their holes, and to hum across the veranda and into the stables. Even they seemed to have no energy. The little square emptied and Richard walked past Sullivan, who saluted him. Richard wanted to change his dusty clothes. Sullivan turned back into the stable and looked over the horses he hated, Slingsby looked over the empty square and waited.

5

Jan eased himself up a little and Anders looked across at him. The sound of the convoy was closer now. In seconds they'd appear round the bluff. Now the commando must contain itself. Anders smiled at Jan and patted his rifle. Jan didn't smile. He looked round at Piet and saw that the boy was still afraid. The boy wouldn't look at him.

A soldier stepped round the bluff and then another and then another. The scouts had made their fatal error and ridden in closer to the column and now they were all in sight. Jan looked again at the boy who was holding his rifle at the ready. His knuckles were white, but he wasn't yet pressing the trigger. Jan knew the boy was a fine shot, but it had to be timed for the right moment. Under his hip he could feel a jagged stone biting into him. His ankle ached and the bandoleer was a weight across his back. Jan lay flat and followed the column towards the river along the sights of his rifle. That would be the leader of the convoy — on the horse. But now another. Two officers and a gun and all the rest. Jan smiled for a moment. He would take the man on the big horse. He hoped the horse wouldn't be killed, she looked a fine animal. He'd take her.

His stomach knotted in anticipation. Below them, and not two hundred yards from them, the gun was being hauled slowly along the track, the man cursing and shouting at the mules. Jan saw the animals heave forward as they smelt water.

The men quickened, the scouts and the officers on their horses moved faster.

Piet watched with wonder as the soldiers marched to the river. No one broke for the water. No one wavered out of the line of march. They might have been going to

25

march right through the water. Like Moses and the Israelites, he thought, and then he heard a shouted order and the men stopped. A man on foot saluted the man on the smaller horse and then turned to the men and shouted something. The *rooineks* broke ranks and ran for the water.

Jan sighted on the other officer and shot him. For a moment the soldiers thought it was a mistake and that they had heard nothing. And then a crashing volley from above them on the bare and deserted hillside showed them their mistake.

Jan had warned the commandos not to shoot the mules, as they would be needed to haul the gun. He had told Piet to take merely the front one on his side. That would stop the gun team from moving. Piet fired and the mule slipped over into the water. The soldiers were running for cover. The Boer commando was deadly accurate.

Lieutenant Willoughby cursed his luck and shouted for Sergeant Rowan. He ordered him to regroup in a square on the other side of the crossing.

'What about you, sir?'

'I'll take three men, we'll break the gun.' Willoughby knew the Boer wanted that above all.

Willoughby and his men were covered by the fire from the soldiers on the other side of the river as they raced for the gun. Jan saw what the man was doing.

'Those, get those,' he shouted and the Wielver Commando poured its fire into the area around the limber.

Willoughby and his men seemed impervious to the fire. They ran, regardless of danger, and reached the gun. Two of the men had taken up axes and were already hacking the gun loose from the limber, another was tugging at the breechblock. Piet shot him through the lungs and he screamed a jet of blood. Willoughby pulled the dying man aside and ripped out the breech-block. As he staggered off the limber the men with the axes finished their work, heaved the gun off and left it with smashed wheels and blockless, a useless lump of metal. The two men helped Willoughby to cross the river and the mud bank on the other side. Bullets plopped into the mud around them. Willoughby felt the man beside him stiffen and drop. His neck was a red pit. The Cotswolds had formed a square and were on rapid fire in their turn.

Willoughby looked about him and saw the sergeant lying dead behind the front line of the square. Two men lay on the river bank and beyond the river lay the wreck of the gun, a scout and his horse, and also the neighing, struggling shape of Rupert Saunders' horse.

Jan Meyer cursed all the gods and prophets and shot the fine horse to relieve it from pain. The gun would be useless to them, he knew. It was broken beyond repair. They'd been good men who did that, he admitted.

He looked over to Piet who looked back at him and smiled. His first blood — good God knows how much more he must shed before it is over, this war. Jan Meyer looked at the men who were still firing into the hillside. They would hit no man from the Wielver Commando today. Jan was too exposed to a serious attack in this position to risk remaining there any longer. It had been worth a desperate attempt and it had failed.

A movement caught his eye. Behind the dead horse, the officer was trapped. He moved his white hand trying to attract the attention of the men on the other side of the river. They didn't see him.

Willoughby moved his men in good order away from the river and the ambush. There was nothing he could do for any of his dead. He had the wounded to carry and supplies and dispatches to take to D Company. These were essential. To attack the Boer would be to face another trap. He left the Kaapshe River as the sun dipped and the shadows grew longer. Tomorrow, when the sun was up, the birds would begin their work.

The flies floated lazily down from the hillside away from the living men and lay fatly on the blood of the man by the gun. Some shone green and blue, guzzling in the neck of the man who had helped Lieutenant Willoughby. There was a gentle buzzing over the valley.

SEARCH

1

Willoughby stood by the window of D Company HQ and looked out at the square. His men were sitting under the shade given by the only tree for miles. They deserved to rest, he thought. Five dead and a number wounded, two in a very bad state indeed.

He felt remote, detached from the incident, somehow. At one moment it had been a routine though hard task, and the next he was dealing with a holocaust. The fire from the hills had gone on, it seemed, for hours and yet the whole engagement was over within three minutes.

James Willoughby was so tired, he knew he would sleep if he sat down. Slingsby looked at him across his desk which had nothing on it. His thin moustache, sharp eyes and cropped hair reeked efficiency and disapproval. Willoughby knew that the Captain was waiting for him to turn before he began the post mortem.

James could see the soldier leaning over the breech of the gun and his mouth spurting blood All he wanted to do was to be sick and then to sleep. He turned round and faced Captain Slingsby and Richard Gaunt, his friend. The room was still and very hot.

They had arrived, after a forced march through the night, at eleven in the morning. The sun was thudding down on them as they marched across the square. A dishevelled, broken column, which had failed to deliver either the weapon or the ammunition with which they had struggled so far.

'Sit down, Lieutenant,' said Slingsby. James shook his head.

'No, I'd prefer to stand, if you don't mind.'

The Captain shrugged and took a pad and a pencil from the desk. Another damned report to write. Slingsby could already feel the sweat rising on his palms.

'Now, tell us again, and slowly, Lieutenant Willoughby. Slowly.'

For the third time, he told the story. He tried to give an idea of what the ambush had been like. It was confused in his mind and he contradicted himself.

'Look, for heaven's sake, can I help it if I didn't remember last time I told you? Yes, I know you have to have it accurate for the report.'

Willoughby could feel himself beginning to break. He was so tired.

'You had scouts riding forward?' Richard asked. Willoughby nodded. 'And they didn't see any sign of the Boer?' Richard was doubtful. Willoughby looked at him angrily.

'They didn't see them. No. The enemy didn't exactly parade his presence. Would you, Richard?'

Richard shook his head and walked across to the shutters. He opened them. Willoughby could feel his legs shaking with fatigue.

'We had a convoy to get across that river, the men were thirsty, tired. They'd been six days —'

'You'd all been six days, Lieutenant Willoughby.' Captain Slingsby's voice reminded him. James nodded.

'We had all been out for six days. The men were thirsty, edgy too.' Slingsby looked up. He was eager for reasons. Willoughby shook his head. 'No, no trouble, Captain Slingsby. None. They just wanted it finished. We came to the river and I had promised that they could break ranks for a time. They needed to have water, a rest.'

Willoughby didn't understand why he was justifying himself. As if he were guilty of some crime. He didn't feel guilty. Did he?

'Five of our men killed.' Slingsby looked up at Willoughby with expressionless blue eyes. Richard turned from the other side of the room where he had been studying the map of the area.

'Our ammunition boxes lost to the enemy.'

'I've already explained —'

'And Captain Saunders is missing.' Richard crossed the room to the desk and stood by it. Slingsby just sat and waited.

'We brought in the wounded. Clare and Mallory and the rest were killed in the first volley.'

'And Sergeant Rowan dead?' Richard would not let go.

Willoughby could see again the broken shape of the sergeant. A bundle of blood, rags and tubes. No more. He nodded.

'Yes, Richard, he is dead.'

Slingsby looked at his notes and sat back in the chair.

'Before, you said Captain Saunders was dead, James.' Willoughby walked slowly to a chair and leaned on it.

'Did I? I forget.'

'You distinctly said "dead".' Slingsby pushed the pad forward for him to see. 'Look.' Willoughby did not bother to move. He shook his head to clear it.

'I don't remember,' he said.

'You told me he was missing.' Richard leant forward towards his friend. Willoughby wanted to hurt Richard suddenly. He felt he was being attacked again, and he was not prepared to be attacked by friends.

'Are you accusing me of something, Richard?'

'No, of course not.'

'Saunders was last seen trapped under his horse. The other side of the river. The Boer side. His horse was dead. Shot dead. He — well — we couldn't see him.'

Willoughby gave a helpless gesture with his left hand.

'He was probably dead, you'd say?' the Captain leaned across his desk.

'Yes.'

'You didn't go back?' Willoughby knew now why he felt defensive, upset, angry. He felt guilty. He had, perhaps, wanted Saunders to be missing. He sighed and shook his head.

'We couldn't go back. They were pouring fire down from the hills. I'd men to regroup. Dispatches and supplies to bring here.'

'I see.' Richard's face was quite still. He showed no sign of emotion, no accusation, but James Willoughby felt it there in his words.

'Are you insinuating something, Richard?' Richard shook his head.

'No, of course not, James. Relax.'

'It sounded uncommonly as though you were.' Willoughby was angry and the blood surged upward for a moment. Richard was the voice of sweet reason. He turned to Captain Slingsby.

'I'm pointing out that we can't be certain he is dead. Not yet.'

'Then go and damned well look and to hell with you,' shouted Willoughby and he sat down.

Slingsby smiled for the first time. He watched the two young men and waited. Nothing happened for a moment and then Richard took his eyes off Willoughby and stood straighter. He did not show a thing in his face. Like his bloody old man, thought Slingsby. It's in his blood.

Slingsby stood up and came from behind his desk.

'James, a long sleep for you and some rest. All right?' He turned to Richard. 'You'll see to the men, Richard. Be sure they get extra rations and as much sleep as they need. Go lightly on their duties for two days.'

32

Richard nodded. Slingsby turned back to the map and began to study it. Without turning round, 'I think that's all gentlemen. You may carry on.'

The two young men went out. Slingsby sighed, opened the collar of his jacket and watched two termites burrowing minute pieces of wood from the top of his desk.

Willoughby lay on the truckle bed and stared at the ceiling. He didn't want to talk to anyone. He wanted to be left to himself for a time.

He was practised, now, at shutting away feelings and any sign of emotions, but Richard had touched something in that interview. He sighed and tried to convince himself that he could not have gone back for Saunders under any circumstances. He was as sure as dammit that the man was dead. Hadn't he been lying under his horse and wouldn't he have made a sign if he had been alive? What a damned nuisance that man had been. And even now he was making trouble, Willoughby cut short that train of thought. But he was certain that, had Saunders been lying on this bed, he'd have felt total indifference to Willoughby lying out there in the cracked mud at the edge of a river.

Richard walked into his room and began to strip off. Willoughby watched him through half open eyes. Richard seemed tense, angry even.

'I couldn't go back, Richard,' Willoughby said. Richard merely turned and looked at him for a moment and then went on changing.

'There must have been ten of them. Up on the hill overlooking the ford. We couldn't go back over the river.' Willoughby wanted to justify his actions, he wanted to be sure that Dorothy never heard anything but the plain truth.

'I'd lost a sergeant and some men, and I had men wounded. I could not go back. And if I couldn't go back,

33

could I ask one of the other men?' Richard shook his head. 'I'm sorry, Richard.' Willoughby meant it.

He raised himself on an elbow and felt his eyes swimming. He lay back again. The damned heat had got to him. He wanted to be sick again.

'Have you been under Boer fire, Richard, like that?' he asked.

Richard shook his head again. Willoughby knew that he would never convince Richard, until he had experienced the murderous power of those ragged troops in action.

'They're only farmers, after all.' Willoughby felt that he could read Richard's mind.

'They're the best shots in the world. And the fastest,' he said. It seemed a lame reason for a soldier not to look for a man who might only have been trapped by his horse. Only another man who had been under that firepower would understand. Slingsby didn't know, Richard didn't know and Willoughby supposed that Dorothy would never know either. He slumped back on the bed.

Richard washed his sunburned face, smoothed down his fair hair and began to strop his razor on the leather by the wash-stand. Soon his face was covered with soap and his blue eyes sparkled as he looked into the small mirror in his case. He hadn't spoken a word since he came into the room.

Outside, Sergeant Holly called a platoon to attention and marched them off for target practice in the veldt. Three men detailed to get water from the well were filling a large container on the wall of the company building. They were larking about with the water and laughing. It was the first laughter that Willoughby had heard since he left Headquarters.

'Are you sure he was dead, James?' Richard was surprisingly gentle when he asked the question. He didn't look round from his shaving.

'I mean, I do understand that you couldn't go back. I'm not attacking you, believe me.'

Richard had become physically mature. His shoulders were a horsemen's shoulders and the muscle had hardened along the back and down the arms. His hair was bleached white by the sunshine and his fair skin was burned red and raw where the collar of his uniform chafed the neck. Willoughby felt suddenly very moved at the sight of the young man, soon to be subjected to the horror of this war. He shuddered at the memory of that soldier tearing at the breech of the gun. It was all so fast and there was blood all over the limber and the ground about them, and Willoughby remembered suddenly that he had pulled that man away from the gun even as he was drowning in his own blood. He'd pushed him aside and left him, with the blood pumping across the ground, like a slit pig. He looked at the back of Richard's head and tried to imagine —

It was all very well for Kitchener and the rest to talk about containing the Boer force. To talk about building blockhouses at strategic points; to order wider and wider sweeps of the country to force the Boer commandos back and up country, to the less hospitable areas away from their own lands. It was all fine talk to think that the problem could be solved by putting women and children into camps, away from their farms on the veldt. Hadn't he even considered deporting all the women to the Dutch East Indies? And the children as well. And certainly Kitchener had known the horrors of the sort of engagement he, James Willoughby, had experienced only two days ago. But to ask a man like Richard Gaunt to do it, to blood him in this frightful way —

Willoughby could suddenly see Richard, at the age of seven, on a pony in the Gloucestershire countryside near his home. He could hear the bugles and the baying of hounds and he turned his face to the wall as he saw in his mind the tail of a fox dipped in its own blood and wiped over the eager face of the young child. Across the breech of the gun a man screamed and blood fountained over his body. Willoughby rubbed the back of his hands on the bed and shivered.

'Richard, I did all I could do,' he said.

Richard nodded and towelled his face and turned to him.

'I'm sorry, James. Of course. Of course you did. Get some sleep, eh?' Richard pulled on his shirt and a jacket and buttoned them up. He walked out into the soft evening and Willoughby lay in a dull daze on the damp blankets.

2

Saunders felt the rough blankets first and then saw a small boy looking down on him. The boy's face was tense and angry and his eyes were like black beads. Low down at his side, Saunders saw the dim light in the room glint on something metallic.

The boy leaned forward and watched as Saunders tried to move. The weight of the blankets seemed like the weight of his horse and he had no strength left. If the boy was going to use the knife, then Rupert Saunders knew that he had no way of preventing it. He lay with his eyes wide, speechless and waited for the blade. The boy stared at his open eyes and stopped. Outside a horse snickered softly, a cow lowed somewhere in the distance.

Saunders heard a crow calling and he shuddered. He knew what these birds did to dead men. Hadn't he seen the dead from the ambush only hours after, and hadn't the birds been thick on them? Tearing, rending, pecking at those sacks of clothes.

Another horse moved and neighed impatiently. There seemed to be a number of them outside. Saunders became aware of a grinding ache in his shoulder. It burned inside as if someone had branded him.

Still the boy watched him. He hadn't blinked. His shock of black hair was roughly cut, his clothes simple and clean, his body already hardened. His small mouth tense and afraid and Saunders knew that, provided he was not surprised or angered, the boy would not use the knife on him. But he had wanted to and Saunders was cold at the thought of it.

The only light that came into the rough room was through a window high in the wall. The walls themselves were of timber. Between the timbers, the cracks were patched with mud and mosses. The whole place seemed to be clean and neat.

Saunders tried to smile at the child, but the boy just stood, unmoving. There was no longer any pretence at concealing the knife. It was in the open between them. A skinning knife, a hunter's knife, and this boy only eleven or so. They grow up to be men early here, Saunders thought. He smiled again and the black eyes of the boy watched him.

Beyond the shut door, Saunders became aware of the dull murmur of voices. Nothing he could understand, but at least the commando was still here.

They had brought him, he remembered, from the river. They had killed his horse and the older men had wanted to kill him. It would be a kindness, they said. To leave him alive here, wounded in the shoulder and with a badly twisted leg where the horse had fallen, would be a slow way to die. Saunders could remember hearing them talking about him as if he were a deer they had found, but were too burdened to carry home. He had heard them in the red haze of his pain and he had forced his eyes open.

They had been looking down at him, a circle of bearded faces with broad-brimmed hats and, above them, the deeper blue of the evening sky.

He could remember hearing the cries of the carrion birds and he remembered also the sweet stink of decay. He had been sick, and they had watched him at their feet as he vomited over himself. They had not moved to help him, they had just watched.

'Kill him, Jan. Is he any use to us?' the tall man had pleaded. 'I will do it now. It will be quicker this way than dragging him through the veldt with a leg and a wounded shoulder like that.'

Saunders lay on his back and tried to remember as much Afrikaans as he had managed to learn. It was hard to remember through the pain, but he knew he had to understand or they would kill like any wounded pony.

The young man, Jan, who was their leader looked at him. He had not made up his mind. Saunders tried to speak.

Jan had shaken his head a little at him. Saunders lay back exhausted on the cracked earth.

'We shall take him,' he said.

'No!' said Anders. 'We have not time. After this ambush, d'you think the British will not send out search parties?' Jan had shrugged.

'We cannot take him. We have no spare animals.'

Another of the old men shook his rifle to make clear how he felt. He wanted to get the killing over and then to be away into the veldt. The British were too close already for comfort.

Already some of the commando leaders had been taken. Some, indeed, had been hanged at the Cape as traitors. They were not men to use such legalistic methods, but if that was the way of the *rooinek*, so be it. And this man lying at their feet was nothing to him.

Jan was determined to take the officer now. He felt that Truus, his wife, would have abominated the idea of killing him as he lay there. To talk of wounded animals in traps would mean nothing to her. God would be avenged, she would say, and Jan was ready to believe it.

'We take him.' And he looked around the group of men to see which would say no. For a moment Anders wanted to argue with him, but finally he said nothing.

He turned away from the black eyes of his commandant and began to search for bullets to fit his rifle from the ammunition of the dead men lying by the bank of the river.

It had taken three days, by difficult trails, to reach Rietsplaas with the British officer strapped to his saddle. There was no spoor for any to follow and they should be safe at Rietsplaas for a few days' rest.

Rupert Saunders looked up again at the boy standing over the bed and he saw in his eyes the hardness of his father. Those black eyes and the curving blade of the knife held close for him to see.

The door opened and Jan Meyer came into the room, crossed to his son and wrenched the knife from his hand. He took it by blade and handle and snapped it across his knee like kindling.

'Piet,' he said, 'go to your mother.' Piet went to the door.

'And Piet, when he is your prisoner, you decide. He is mine and I will say what happens with him. You will not have the killing of him.'

'You told me, Papa, you told me a man like him was at the killing of my grandfather. Your father. You told me that.' The boy was frightened. He knew that his father was angry with him under his calmness.

'Yes,' Jan said, 'yes, he was shot by them early in this war and yes, by a man like this man. But this man is mine and my father was mine. You will not avenge him, that is for me, Piet.' Piet was surprised to see tears in the eyes of his father and he walked out of the room.

Jan looked at Saunders. Saunders sighed and shut his eyes. He wanted to sleep now, more than anything. Jan left the small room and shut the door.

Piet stood by his mother at the open fireplace. The roughly cut stones that formed the mantle and the surround were polished by years of use. Jan looked around the room with some pride. Hadn't they built this place together, Truus and he? The benches he had made and the chairs. There was a Dutch dresser that held the gleaming crockery that Truus had brought from the old country and which was never used. The curtains at the windows were freshly cleaned and the floor well swept. Truus would not allow dogs in here and Jan was proud of her care for Rietsplaas.

'All right, Jan, so now we have this man, what do we do with him?' Anders was irritated and Jan sighed. He did not want arguments, not now. He knew that after such an action their nerves were on edge. He had no wish for hard words with Anders.

The commandos sat round the big table with empty plates in front of them. Jan signalled to Truus to clear the table and she did it quietly, without disturbing the men. She smiled and ruffled the hair of Piet Leyds, but he pulled away from her. Now he, too, was a man. Hadn't he shot the mule and the man trying to get the part from the big gun? His father's gun that had been brought to him was a good gun and his father, lying up in the mountains beyond that river, would be pleased. He watched as Jan stood at the fireplace.

'All right, Jan Meyer, you bring him here, you make us carry him on horses here — and for what? He would have been carrion only, if we had left him, and the British one officer less. Now he is a danger to us all.' Anders looked around at the other men for support and they lifted their heads a little.

They had become tired of letting this *rooinek* ride turn and turn about while they had stumbled across the hard paths that Jan had chosen for their escape. This Saunders, who spoke a little Afrikaans, and who was suffering from bad wounds should, in their minds, have been dead. They did not dare ask Jan while they were marching why they had brought him out. Now Anders was asking and they waited.

Jan shrugged and moved slowly across to the table, until he was very close to Anders. He leaned down to his face and looked at the older man closely.

Anders moved awkwardly in his chair and Jan stared at him.

'Well?' Anders asked.

41

'I have reasons, good reasons. I want him here in my place for my reasons.'

'We should know them,' said Anders. 'We have a right to know them.' He was encouraged by the grumble of assent from the other men around the table.

Jan looked quickly along the line of faces opposite. Piet Leyds, the boy, and Gerry Zwanenburg with his long jaw stared dully at him; de Jong smiled at him and fingered a piece of meat inside his plump mouth; Harry Kraak rubbed his nose and gazed at the ceiling. Jan looked round at Truus who stood with her back to the dresser. She was still holding the dirty dishes in her large hands.

'You are all bigger fools than you seem, if you don't see why Jan brings back an officer.'

The men were surprised when Truus spoke. If their women had spoken in such a way, called their friends fools, then their woman would have been ordered out and maybe beaten later. A woman's place was to cook, to clean and to have babies. Perhaps because this one could only have one baby she was more willing to speak. More difficult to control.

Jan smiled at her. He had felt it would be right to rescue the officer, but he hadn't known why and now that the man was lying in a bed in his house, it would be hard to take him out and kill him.

Truus knew that Jan was troubled for a reason. She pushed a stray length of her long golden hair away from her face and the men saw the plain marriage ring on her ringer.

Jan Meyer's woman was a woman to beware of. Not one to cross words with, for she had a fine mind and a hard tongue. All of them, even Anders who was no lover of women, admired her. Her body was beautiful and her face was strong. She and Jan had broken this land together, built this house together and they were very close.

Truus walked slowly over to the table, laid the dirty plates down in front of Anders and leaned on the table.

'He is a British officer, ja?' She leaned on the knuckles of her hands. 'He is wounded, ja? He comes from Pretoria.'

She rocked back and forth as she spoke and suddenly she straightened upright.

'And you do not know his use to us. You are fit for nothing but digging the earth and eating worms, you.' She smiled at them to soften her words and they watched her.

'He is a prisoner and we can bargain with him.' They still did not understand.

'We have many held in their camps, some to be tried in their courts in the Cape. Very well, we have, then, a man we can use as barter.'

Jan smiled, walked away from the table and dipped for some water from the covered jar in the corner of the room. Then the others understood. Even Anders nodded and sat back and picked his teeth.

Truus walked slowly back to Jan and he offered her his cup of water. She took it, drank and smiled with her eyes across the rim of the cup, because she knew that she had made it possible for him to lead the commandos again.

Anders got up from the table and went across to Truus and Jan.

'Mevrou, I thank you for the food,' he said.

'You should thank God,' Truus reminded him. He nodded and went back to the table. They all stood with bowed heads and Jan thanked God for the food and for their safety.

Anders and the rest then moved away from the table and de Jong agreed to take first turn on picket. The others went silently to their beds in the barn, or wrapped themselves in blankets out under the stars.

Jan nodded to Piet and the boy went to his small room. He had said nothing. Jan dropped the latch of the soldier's room and put out the lamp.

Truus was already lying in the big wooden bed, as he washed, for the first time in ten days. He sat on the hard edge of the bed and pulled at his boots. His ankle was swollen and ached where it was too tight. He took his knife, slit the leather over the instep and slid the boot away. The new boots lay as he flung them and he turned to Truus, who waited for him with a laughing face.

When they had made love she was still laughing and Jan lay quiet by her side.

'What is so funny, Truus?'

'You,' she said, 'you are very funny. I knew that you didn't know what to do with that man. I knew it.' Jan laughed too. He was a lucky man to have such a woman.

'And when we go, will you be able to manage with him?'

She rolled over quickly. 'Go?'

Jan reached for her hand and she pulled it away. 'Why? The land needs men now. Water is scarce and a woman cannot carry as much as is needed. The farm must have you now.'

Jan shook his head. 'Piet will be with you,' he said. Truus was angry. She knew that her man was a good man and that he was kind too, but she knew that he had a pain to burn out of himself, an anger, a vengeance to wreak and nothing could prevent it.

'Vengeance is mine, saith the Lord.'

And Jan had said, 'It is mine also. For my father's death I will fight.'

Truus knew that the Wielver Commando would be leaving after a day or two. She sighed and took his hand. 'I can manage him,' she said. Jan shut his eyes and slept.

44

3

The morning sun was still not too strong and Richard answered the salute from Sergeant Holly with a smile.

'Morning, Sergeant Holly. Good night?'

'Morning, sir. Thank you, yes. Captain Slingsby sends his compliments and would you be kind enough to step over to his quarters, sir.'

Richard was surprised that Slingsby should want to see anyone so early in the morning and in his own quarters at that. He was a shy man and rarely, if ever, could Richard remember being summoned to Slingsby's room.

'Thank you, Sergeant Holly.'

Richard walked across the square and knocked on the door.

'Come in.' Richard went into the dim room and saw that Slingsby was half dressed and shaving. The room was too hot and stuffy, as if no windows had been opened during the night. An orderly was holding the mug of warm water for Slingsby to dip his brush.

'Get out, Taylor,' Captain Slingsby ordered and the orderly went like a rabbit.

'Sit down somewhere, Richard. Excuse my asking you over this time in the — look here, I want a private word. All right?'

Richard nodded. He had already guessed what Slingsby wanted.

'Saunders.' Slingsby took off a swathe of white soap. He flicked it into the bowl. Richard waited.

'D'you think he was killed?' Richard didn't say anything.

'Well?'

Richard looked about the room. He could smell the

soap that Slingsby was using. 'I don't know,' he said.

'No more do I.' Slingsby turned round to face Richard. 'The others all have the same story. No one could've gone across the river into the Boer guns to find out.' Richard nodded.

'I believe that, sir. Don't you?'

Slingsby looked at Richard. 'He's a friend of yours, Richard.'

'I don't think I understand what you mean.'

Slingsby whisked up some more lather and dabbed it on his face.

'He said the guns were firing. He said that no one could see Saunders. He said the horse Saunders had been riding was hit.'

Richard stood up. The other men say it too.' Slingsby nodded and nicked himself.

'Damn it. You do believe him, then.'

'Willoughby may be a friend of mine,' Richard said. 'But Rupert Saunders is married to my cousin. A relative.'

Slingsby nodded. He wiped off the remains of the soap and dried his face with a towel. He threw the towel on to the bed and smiled across at Richard.

'Yes. I know. Thought you might like to go and look. See what you can see. Take a small patrol. Sergeant Holly. Have a look, follow them up.'

Richard waited. Slingsby pulled on his jacket and walked to the door. He checked in a mirror on a nail on the back of the door and opened the door for Richard.

'All right?'

Richard nodded.

'Yes. Naturally. Follow them up?'

'We'll talk in my office. Just wanted your agreement in principle. I'm awaiting a reply to a message telegraphed to HQ. In an hour, then. Get some breakfast down you. Decide who you want to take.'

Richard walked out of Slingsby's quarters and on to the veranda. He walked to the long hitching post outside the house and stroked the muzzle of one of the ponies standing in the shade of the house. What the devil was Slingsby cooking up, he wondered.

He slowly crossed the dusty square and opened the door of the men's quarters. He went inside and the men lying about there looked up. Inspection was over and this was a half hour of the morning they could usually call their own.

Richard looked through the gloom to the far end of the building and saw Holly emerging from his cubicle.

'Sar'nt!' Richard called.

'Sir?' Holly saluted smartly for the second time that day. The men watched, disinterested. Most of them were used to obeying orders and never asking the whys and wherefores, and that was how the British Army liked them.

Richard Gaunt was a funny kettle of fish and that was the truth of it. Didn't he sometimes ask them to think for themselves, even to ask questions? They knew, the old sweats, that the time would come when he'd nail someone to the floor for asking a question, or for using his initiative.

Most of the men were young, with just a sprinkling of older hands. The regular men were the older ones and the rest had been taken on for the war. They didn't like or dislike it. It gave them a roof over their heads, sometimes, and food in their bellies, such as it was. And you saw a thing or two and didn't have worries. That was for the officers, like young Gaunt.

Sullivan lay back on the hard pallet and looked at Richard talking to Sergeant Holly. He chewed on a piece of dried meat and watched the two men. Something was up. And it didn't take much guessing to know that it was to do with the convoy that had been shot to bits. Hadn't

47

they lost a bloody field-gun, and that a valuable piece of equipment?

Sullivan laughed at the thought of the quartermaster at Headquarters, when he came to check his stores. No one had signed for it this end, except with blood, and it was signed out at his place. So who had the responsibility, on whose manifest should it appear?

Sullivan chewed over the problem and the meat about equally and wondered why he'd ever joined this rat-bag of an army. To be kicked from pillar to post by Holly and him no better'n a parson's toe rag; to be shouted at by Slingsby or asked to think by that boy over there. He swung his legs off the bed and stood up as Sergeant Holly called his name.

'Sullivan, Crow, Spring, Anderson, McCarthy, Hughes —' Holly reeled off a list of names and the men stood up as they were called. Richard walked down the stables and looked at each man. He nodded and smiled and walked on. Sergeant Holly gave orders as Richard looked at the men chosen to come with him to the scene of the ambush. A quick reconnaissance should be sufficient. They would be quicker on foot over the rough country to the river crossing.

'. . . outside in half an hour with full marching order. Rations will be drawn by you, Crow, and you, Hughes. For six days.' Richard turned round.

'Three days, Sergeant.' The Sergeant nodded and changed the order.

'Thirty minutes, Sergeant,' Richard said and walked out of the stables.

A buzz of speculation followed him and he smiled at it. At last they were seeing something other than the routine they were so bored with. They'd look livelier now, perhaps, and sharpen up with their lives at risk out across the veldt towards the mountains.

Richard stood and looked beyond the black shape of

the trees at the end of the square. As far as he could see, the veldt stretched away to the east. And to the north the land was soft and more mysterious with sudden hollows and dips. A rolling, soft land, like inland Devon almost.

He could almost see the stream he had fished as a boy, and the house in Gloucestershire, with the peaches on the wall of the kitchen garden. He could hear the barking of the dogs and the sound of a carriage and pair on gravel as it turned in at the drive. And his father, in full dress, with medals a rainbow of colours on his chest, striding down the steps into the sunken garden. He could see his mother running to greet her husband and the laughing and crying and the parties they made. Sometimes Dorothy would come up from the vicarage in South Devon. Now Richard's father was dead and his mother out here, nursing somewhere with Dorothy. And even Charlotte was here too, and the last he remembered of her was as a girl with long curls and a serious face. It all seemed a long time ago.

Across the land the heat was shimmering off the earth. Made drowsy by the sun, the birds had stopped calling in the trees.

Jenkins, his orderly, walked across the square holding the reins of his pony. It was a tougher beast than it looked and suited to the sort of country they would be passing through. Richard hurried across to the company office to see what final thoughts Slingsby had about this sortie into the hills. It would be well to be on the march before James woke from his sleep. He didn't want to be embarrassed by explaining that Slingsby had wanted to check up on the situation at the ford.

The wreck of the field-gun lay where it had been when Jan Meyer and his men had left the river crossing. A black bird sat on one of the shattered wheels and cocked his head. It was afternoon and the heat was waning. Beyond the gun and its limber was the bloated

49

body of a horse. Already it had rotted and formed gases and stank. Already the mouth was open in a rictus and a fly was crawling from under the dry tongue. A stream of ants paraded through the gleaming sockets of the eyes, burrowing slowly into the gristly passages of the skull.

A man lay near the limber where he had fallen, surrounded by black blood and feathers, where the birds had squabbled over titbits from the body.

Richard and his party looked down the slopes and imagined the way the battle had happened.

'Jesus wept,' muttered Sergeant Holly. Richard stood silent and reflected on the real rewards of the war.

'Bury them,' he ordered.

4

In the dining-room of the hotel they could hear the soft sounds of music. Laughter and the tinkle of glasses floated across the room and disturbed Dorothy as she sat and toyed with her ice. Mrs Gaunt was laughing at something Lord Lake had said and Dorothy admired her poise and her determination. Some had said she was too old to uproot herself and to nurse the soldiers. Some had said she was becoming gaga since the death of her husband, but that was hardly true.

Dorothy smiled and looked around the table. The dinner had been a fine one, the wine was French and, somehow, being guests of Lord Lake and his family had given them all an added zest. They had been growing into dull dogs, she thought.

Charlotte's dark hair set off the white of her neck and shoulders to perfection. Once she had been a vivacious, gay girl, but out here she had seen too much, heard too much, and waited too long for death. Men she nursed with frightful injuries did die, even though they were heroes, and death is a surprise to a young girl.

Dorothy knew that Charlotte was beginning to have nightmares about seeing her brother, Richard, being brought into the operations room and adding one of his limbs to the pile. Dorothy ate the last biscuit and smiled at Lord Lake's young son, who seemed to be a Lieutenant in a fashionable regiment from his dress uniform.

'Doin' jolly well, my boy,' the old man had boomed across the room when they were all introduced earlier that evening. 'And gettin' in a spot of huntin' too eh, Andrew, eh?'

The boy nodded, embarrassed by his father. Dorothy had felt an instant sympathy for him. Perhaps he was in awe of the old man and no wonder, she thought. He was formidable. The cropped white hair and the huge face over the evening dress, the large hands more used to handling whips and reins than knives and forks, the soft mouth that laughed as loudly as it talked. Dorothy wasn't sure that she disliked the man on sight, but after this meal with him she was sure, now, that he was no good for the young man sitting opposite Charlotte. He never allowed the boy to finish a sentence or to have an idea of his own and Dorothy knew that Charlotte would be far from impressed by the handsome face or the beautiful uniform. Wasn't she here in South Africa out of a sense of duty? Or was it because her mother wanted her to forget that dreadful Socialist young man with the red hair? Wasn't she here to work and not to sit over dinner in large hotels? Wasn't she here to support her brother, who was somewhere up the country fighting? She would never be impressed by such a young man and Dorothy was sorry for him.

'Will you be dancing this evening, Mrs Saunders?' he asked and she was surprised at the question.

'Dancing?' she asked.

'We thought of popping along to the dancing after dinner. Father likes to look at the ladies, and I thought maybe Miss Charlotte might care to take a turn or two. And that perhaps you –.' His voice trailed off as Dorothy shook her head.

'I'm sorry,' she said, 'I'm afraid I haven't danced for — oh! A very long time.'

Dorothy regretted it. She regretted that, since her marriage with Rupert, they had never once danced together.

He disliked dancing and regarded it as a damned insufferable bore and he said so at every opportunity. Dorothy loved it and suffered in silence. It wasn't much to give up for a marriage, she had thought. But how she

52

envied the girls their dancing. The excitement of dressing, the carriage waiting, the chaperon and the final instructions from mamma — the music and the laughing and the dresses and the young men. Lord Lake's son was talking to her again.

'I'm sorry,' she said, 'I haven't heard a word you've said.' He laughed and her confusion vanished.

He had fine eyes and a well-shaped head and Dorothy found herself wanting to dance. Perhaps the French wine —

'I wondered if I could mark your card myself?' he repeated.

'I'm sure Charlotte would rather I did not —.'

'By all means, Dorothy. Why ever not? You never seem to dance. Rupert doesn't like you to, I suppose' Charlotte was direct to the point of rudeness.

'I shall stay outside, thank you,' Dorothy said. 'I feel in need of air.'

She could see that Mrs Gaunt was annoyed with her and that Lord Lake thought her a dull fish, but Dorothy was not concerned by what they thought.

She sat by a window and the soft light from the single lamp glowed on the polished carved wood of the mantelshelf, the mahogany of the huge armchairs. She was alone in the quiet room and, in the distance, she could hear the music.

5

Willoughby was angry. Damned angry, and he made it very clear.

'You don't believe me, do you? Not a damned word I say.'

'Keep your voice down, James,' snapped Slingsby. 'You'll be heard across the square.'

'D'you think I give a damn who hears me?' He stormed up to the desk where Slingsby sat and leaned over it. James was a big man and Slingsby sat like a bantam and waited for the younger man to subside. Richard stood unhappily near the windows and said nothing. James turned on him.

'You too. A friend, and you too. You go and check my report. Well, he was dead, wasn't he? Under his horse. Just as I told you?'

He stopped speaking as he looked at Richard's face. Richard shook his head. James turned back to Captain Slingsby and waited for an explanation.

'Well?' he asked.

Tell the Lieutenant, Mr Gaunt,' said Slingsby.

'He wasn't there,' said Richard. I'm sorry, James, but Rupert Saunders was not under his horse, he was not in the valley. There was no sign. Not of him.'

James Willoughby sat down. He wasn't sure what to say nor even what to think.

'He must have been there. I saw his horse fall —. He must have been there.'

'No,' said Richard. 'We buried them, the ones who were there. D'you think we don't know who we buried?'

'Then where — ?' Willoughby began.

'There were signs that he had been taken away, Lieutenant. Carried away. Men had dragged him from under the horse and taken him. He must, therefore, have been alive, captured, Willoughby. Rupert Saunders must be held by the Boer,' said Slingsby. 'No one is blaming you. Lieutenant. You did what was right, no doubt of that.'

Willoughby smiled bitterly at them both.

'Not now you've checked the place.'

'Precisely,' said Slingsby. 'Precisely.' He looked at the two young men before him.

Such different young men and so angry with each other. Richard Gaunt, smart, fair haired, soft almost, and impeccably descended. James Willoughby rounder, taller, more comfortable apparently, but with the pain of experience etched in every crease of his face. A man more like himself, Slingsby thought, bitterly. His mouth twitched and clamped still as a trap. An orderly knocked on the door.

At last the men might have some real action. Slingsby was almost grateful to the Boer Commando who had taken Captain Saunders, whom he disliked anyway. They might make it possible for D Company to move out of these damned buildings, into action.

'Come in,' he barked and the messenger stepped in smartly enough, saluted and handed across a dispatch from HQ. Slingsby dismissed him with a nod and slit open the dispatch.

The two men watched him. They dared not look at each other. Their anger would take time to go.

'Well, gentlemen,' he said, when he had read the dispatch. 'At last. At last we'll have the men off their backsides. Do 'em good. A bit of action.' Slingsby grinned. The dispatch from Battalion Headquarters left no doubt as to the action he could initiate.

'When, sir?' asked Richard. Slingsby handed him the dispatch and Richard scanned it quickly before handing it back.

Slingsby put it on the desk, where Willoughby could

see it if he chose to. Slingsby looked at Richard's face. Richard asked too many questions and thought too much about the consequences of his actions. He would have to learn not to, or he would never make the soldier his father had been.

Slingsby picked up the dispatch again. He read it over. '"To D Company. Warning order stop. You will carry out search and burn all farms in vicinity of the Kaapshe River crossing. No move before dawn October 17th".' Slingsby looked up at Richard. 'D Company will implement the order, Gaunt, with relish, I trust.'

Richard had no wish to burn farms nor to implement the orders. He turned back to face the other two officers. They knew, from his grim face, what he felt about such orders and they waited for his reaction.

Willoughby wandered across to the window and sat down on the sill.

'They hardly fight like gentlemen, eh, Richard?' He grinned sardonically as he said it and looked out across the mud square at the platoons of men exercising there.

Sergeant Holly was shouting orders, while Sullivan watched and nodded to the men who were still filling the water tank. You would never think that, beyond those buildings, a man would as likely be shot as survive. James Willoughby was bitter and it showed.

'They fight like damn savages, Richard. No quarter, no warnings, no honour. You had better know that. You buried those men out there at the crossing. They can hardly have been a pretty sight.' Richard's face tightened at the memory. His eyes shone with the anger he felt.

'I was sick, if you must know, James. But these Boer are not gentlemen, are they? So we can hardly expect them to fight like us, can we?'

Willoughby raised his right hand and looked across the country from the window. Richard turned to Slingsby.

'Dawn tomorrow, then, sir? Will that be all?' he asked and Slingsby smiled his thin smile at him.

'Let us be clear, Gaunt. In case you do find any sign, you know what your orders are?' Richard nodded.

'Well?' asked Slingsby. He was enjoying this. It might toughen up this boy. Might even make a soldier of him.

'We search each farm, sir,' said Richard. His distaste was evident in the way he ground out the words. His disgust at the idea, quite clear from the straightness of his back and the rigidity of his features. Willoughby was almost sorry for him.

'Should we find any trace of a Boer Commando using any farm, we burn it. Farmhouse, outbuildings, all of it.'

Slingsby nodded and pushed the dispatch across the desk to Richard, with the point of a paper knife.

'You'd better take that to stiffen your resolve, Gaunt, Those men were killed by the Boer. Remember that. Remember that, Gaunt, when you set the first farm afire. I will give orders to section commanders in twenty minutes.'

Richard saluted the Captain. He marched for the door as Slingsby beckoned Willoughby over to the desk.

'You're very tired, I've no doubt, James.' Willoughby shook his head. The night's sleep had done him good.

'I understand that Captain Saunders' wife is nursing in an officers' hospital?'

Willoughby nodded. He couldn't answer. His mouth was dry. He waited. Richard had stopped in the doorway and James knew that he was listening. He didn't care now.

'You were due back in HQ in four days. Would you be inconvenienced, Willoughby, by telling Mrs Saunders we're doing all we can?'

Willoughby straightened up and his face was quite impassive. He looked across at Richard, who did not take his eyes off Willoughby. He shook his head, but Willoughby chose to ignore it.

'Why no. Of course,' he said. Slingsby smiled at him and stood.

'Telegraph is so — impersonal, don't you know? Don't raise her hopes too high.'

Willoughby walked out of the room past Richard, aware that he had made an error, aware that he was committing himself to a path that he had forsworn. He was already wondering what Dorothy would say, how she would look, what she would be wearing! He wondered if he would even raise her hopes at all. A wounded man, alone, would be a handicap to a commando. They might well leave him and then he would certainly die. It had happened before.

Maybe Dorothy was already free . . . He knew he must not think such thoughts and he stood in the blazing sun in the middle of the mud square and looked about him, blindly. He had no idea how long he had been standing and looking like this. His mind was seething with thoughts of Dorothy Saunders and he knew a sweet guilt as he stared across the heat-hazed veldt. Already that man could be white bones . . .

6

The Captain was sweating in his narrow bed. Truus knew that. Fever was making him difficult to keep still. Already he had opened the wound through his shoulder, so that it was bleeding again. Truus had re-dressed the wound with help from Joseph, the black boy they kept on Rietsplaas. There was little to do, except let the fever burn itself out and then to hope that the English Captain would have the strength left to make a recovery.

If the wound became infected, he would die anyway and Truus shrugged. Perhaps it would be best, she thought. He will be a burden to us here.

Truus sat on the step in her rocking-chair and watched the chickens pecking for corn in the dust of the yard. They were scraggy birds with naked necks. She shuddered as she thought of the carrion birds up there, in the high veldt.

Jan had ridden off with the rest of the Wielver Commando. They were rested and confident again and they had gone with blessings from her. But Truus was uneasy and had begged her man to stay with her. Let Anders take the group this time. Let any one of the other men take his turn at leading, but each time she asked, Jan smiled at her and asked her if she was afraid for him. And each time, she had to say that she was not afraid for him. But she was. Deep in her stomach a knot stayed and always she thought of her man and of her fear.

He was the only thing in the world for her. Where he stopped so, too, did her life. And with her fear grew an anger against the arrogant, wounded man in the small room at the back of her house.

Truus got up from her chair and walked to a huge tree on the edge of the first field they had broken. Her long serge skirt billowed around her as she walked. The white blouse fitted her well and she knew that she was a fine looking woman. Some of the other wives disliked her. Some said she was brazen. Some that she made too much of her beauty. Some were just jealous, but none dared to say so to her face, for they knew that the tongue of Truus Meyer was unswerving in the Lord.

Each day she read from her husband's Bible, each day she taught her little boy, each day she prayed for her family and for her land and for her man.

The other women in their black dresses and poke bonnets were distorted by bearing a child each year, like cattle, and they were angry because she was not. Because she was barren now, and this meant that she was still a young woman and attractive to the men.

Truus walked and her long hair reached her shoulders where she had let it hang free since her man went with his commando. She had watched the small group ride slowly across the land. As far as the eye could follow them, it was Boer land and she was proud that her man was willing to defend it. She had watched the group ride to the fighting and had held tight the hand of her boy who wanted, already, to go with them.

'If Piet Leyds can go, why can't I? I can shoot better than he can,' he had grumbled. But Jan had said no, and though he had argued, he had stopped when he saw the anger in his father's eyes.

Truus had watched the horsemen go. Their broken hats, the ragged jackets, the old shirts and the heavy, double, bandoleer of cartridges. Truus touched the rough bark of the tree and looked across the long, falling valley. Jan had not looked back at her, or his son. The men of the commando rode stiffly, aware of her watching eye and only little Piet Leyds had looked round and she had waved to him. He had not waved back.

'Behold I say, how they reward us, to come to cast us out of thy possession, which thou hast given us to inherit.'

Truus felt the knot tighten in her stomach and quite suddenly felt a pain such as she had never known, save when bearing her child. She leaned against the tree and then the pain was gone and she was panting from it, like a buck that has run itself out. Truus rubbed her hand across her forehead and felt the sweat starting under the hair at her temples. She stood away from the tree and trembled with weakness.

A crow passed over and she watched its dark shadow, as it soared out over the valley and towards the hills. Her mouth was dry and her tongue forced itself between her lips for a moment. She felt sick with fear. Slowly it passed and then she shook herself, like a dog, and turned to look at Rietsplaas and the farm. The corn was ripe and the vegetables needed water. Already the sun was scorching the earth and Piet had not begun to carry water with Joseph to irrigate the rows of cabbage and potatoes. Truus turned away from the tree.

The house stood quite alone. At one end was the water barrel with a pipe running to it from the roof. The overlapping rough planks that made up the roof were bent and warped by the sun, but they kept out the weather. The planks were knotted and seamed and greyed, so that the house seemed to grow out of the soil like an outcrop of rock.

Around the house was a low veranda with a rail, and most of the rooms had a door on to the veranda as well as a door into the main central room. She had wanted it to be like this and Jan had agreed. The windows had shutters, but no glass. For who could afford to order glass from the town, risk bringing it all these miles and then find that it was broken, or that it did not fit?

In front of the house, a few flowers grew in pots against the struts of the veranda and Truus watered them when she had time.

61

There was a small barn for the cattle in the winter. Now it was full of hay and chickens and sometimes, when Jan was home, his pony would sleep in there. Harness hung from the beams and the soap and brushes for the animals were kept along the shelf at the far end of the barn. Beyond this building was a rickety fence and this spread all round the farm buildings, more as a statement that this was their land than as a fence either to keep things out or to keep things in. Neighbours had laughed at Meyer and his wife for building such a thing out here in the veldt. But it was best to leave Jan Meyer to himself and the same was true of his wife.

But now Trims was lonely for she had no friends to come visiting. All of the women had men away, fighting. Some with Jan, but they had always been afraid of the closeness between Jan and Truus. They were lucky to have found each other. Each was strong and self-reliant in so many ways. Each loved the other more each day and each year that passed.

Truus brushed her hair out of her eyes with strong, brown hands and stomped up the steps into the house.

'Piet,' she called. 'Piet.'

In the dim light that filtered through the shutters, Truus saw Piet standing at the doorway of the small room in which Saunders lay, sweating, on the bed. Piet was whittling a stick with the skinning knife his father had given to him for his last birthday. She knew that he wanted to kill the man. She knew that he hated this Englishman for what his kind had done, and were doing, to the Boer.

She was shocked at the level of hatred in the boy and feared it too. Behind his dark eyes was the same burning hatred that was behind Jan's eyes. She knew that for them all, even when the war was finished, and whoever won it, there would always be hatred and anger. Not only in her and in Jan, but in her child also, and in his

62

children too.

She picked up a pitcher of water and walked past the boy, who continued his whittling. She walked into Saunders' room and looked at the wounded soldier. The sweat poured from his forehead and across his throat to his chest. The bandage covering the wound was stained with fresh blood. Truus sighed. There was little she could do for the man.

Truus wondered what his wife was thinking. She knew that Saunders was married from the miniature he carried in his pocket and from the ring on his finger. These things they had placed carefully on the shelf over his head. Boers do not steal or loot from such men. They are men of honour, she thought, and she put down the miniature. She looked down and saw that he was watching her with unseeing eyes. He groaned and rolled over on to his wounded arm and screamed with the pain, as the jagged bits of bone scraped together.

Piet came quickly into the room.

'Help me!' she ordered. He looked for a moment as if he would refuse. Then he pulled the man roughly across the bed, so that he was lying flat.

'I don't want to help him,' Piet said. 'I don't care if he hurts.'

Truus carefully lowered the body of the Captain who had fainted from the pain. She looked at her fingers, which were stained with the fresh blood on the bandages, and she showed it to Piet.

'It is a man dying here,' she said. 'If your father would ever be shot, if he should be left for dead by his commando, if he should be picked up by the British, you had better pray to the Lord that he is looked after like this. For if he is not, he will surely be dead.'

Piet looked stonily at her and Truus sat on the hard wooden edge of the Captain's bed. How could she explain mercy to this boy, who had already lost his grandfather, whom he loved?

'See this blood?' She showed him again. 'It is the blood of a man. A soldier. He is dying maybe. In a strange place and without anyone he loves near him. It is lonely for him here, with us. We are his enemies and if he dies it will be without ever seeing again his wife, or perhaps his children, and this is his blood.'

'But for soldiers they always die like it, Mother. They always die in the veldt or with other men maybe, or lying by themselves under the sun. It is nothing new this. It is a soldier's life and they choose it. My father doesn't choose it. He has to go to fight the soldiers. My grandfather didn't choose it either. He died because he had to keep the British from our land. War is what this man lives for, isn't it?'

She sighed. The small boy patted her hand.

'Come, clean the hand. It is only a British soldier. Clean it off and give me something to eat, please.'

Truus smiled. Piet was still child enough to think of his stomach. She rubbed the blood from her hand with a cloth and the water from the pitcher. With a little of the water, she moistened the soldier's mouth and wiped his forehead and then she and Piet went out and closed the door.

The fever had to break soon or Saunders would have no strength to build on and he would surely die out in this fierce land. Perhaps only the scaring pain of the shattered bones would keep him alert enough to decide to live. Saunders' mouth puckered open and his tongue dragged in a little of the water Truus had left there on the surface of his skin.

Outside, a dog barked and some chickens with scrawny, pink necks scratched about the yard.

7

Richard dipped the brush into the tepid water and tried to whip up a lather. Willoughby lay back on his bed with his eyes shut, keeping the day out for as long as possible. Richard scraped away. He and James had not spoken since the interview with Slingsby. They had found ways to occupy themselves that did not require any conversation. Richard had come to bed late, after finalizing arrangements for the search-party with Sergeant Holly.

Richard was relieved that Captain Slingsby had suggested that they should split the company and that he should have an opportunity of working on his own. He smiled into the cracked mirror and wiped away the last of the soap.

'Slingsby doesn't like you, old chap. Don't get under his skin.' Willoughby had not opened his eyes and Richard smiled at the oblique overture.

'I try not to,' he said and began to pack his shaving kit in the box provided.

To tell you the truth, he's a self-satisfied bastard.' Willoughby opened one eye and looked at Richard. 'You ready?'

Richard was pulling on his shirt and buttoning it up.

'More or less,' he said and began to check through the kit laid out on his bed by the orderly. Water bottle, belt, sola topee, pistol, holster, lanyard, whistle, small pack, first-aid bandages, spare rounds, flask, field-glasses, watch, compass, handkerchief, pencil.

There was a knock at the door. Willoughby rolled off the bed and sat on the edge.

'Come!' he called and Sergeant Holly stepped smartly in and flashed a salute at Richard.

'Good morning, Sergeant. All ready?' asked Richard. Holly nodded, his cropped head stiff as a marionette's.

'Yes, sir.'

'And the men ?'

'They'll be all right sir, once we get moving, sir.' Holly was sure of his men. The section he had chosen for the lieutenant and himself would be all right. And Captain Slingsby could have the rest and welcome.

'Everyone is clear about what they are to do, Sergeant ?'

'Yes, sir,' said Holly. Did this young whipper-snapper think that Holly left things like that to chance?

Richard pulled on his tunic and looked into the small mirror to fasten the stiff top buttons.

'Just one thing, sir. There are some of the men, sir, who don't rightly like the idea of burning farms down. I'd not meant to say 'owt, but you'd best know I thought —'

Willoughby stood up. He was taller than the sergeant and as broad.

'What on earth d'you mean, Sergeant ?' Richard demanded.

'Not wi' women, and us killin' them too, sir.' The sergeant knew he should not have brought it up now. He cursed his bloody luck and wished he had kept his mouth shut.

'It doesn't matter, sir. Be all right.'

Richard stepped closer to him and Holly could see the anger in his eyes.

'You get out there double-quick, Sergeant, and scotch those rumours. We are killing no women. Make it clear. I'll inspect sections in five minutes. That's all.'

Sergeant Holly saluted and turned for the door, to find his way blocked by Willoughby.

'Sergeant,' he said and Holly stopped still. 'The enemy did kill our men, remember. Our men.'

'Yes, sir. I know, sir. Clare and Mallory were friends of mine, sir. I know that, sir.'

66

'You'd do well, Sergeant, to make sure the rest of the company knows it too.' Willoughby looked down at the sergeant and waited. Holly looked at him for a moment and then left, without a word.

Richard was angry.

'There was no need for that, James.' Willoughby dug out his boots from under the bed and sat down to pull them on.

'I think there was,' he said. 'When the Colonel passes an order to search and destroy, it's the word of God, don't you know.'

Willoughby was mocking the old man and tugging at the «tiff boot as he did so. He smiled up at Richard.

'Orders, Richard, is orders. Whether they come from Kitchener, Roberts, Coote or Slingsby. Orders is —'

'— Orders,' Richard interrupted him. 'Yes, I know. I think. I shall hit the next person who says that to me. I have the feeling that Slingsby actually enjoys the idea of burning farms. I couldn't do it. The waste — the years spent building up fields from — the stock, the crops.'

He thought of razing the home farm to the ground in Gloucestershire. Of hamstringing the cattle and ruining the wells on the farms. He thought of burning the crops and riding down the wheat and oats. He thought of setting fire to barns and he loathed the idea. He loathed James, at that moment, for he was smiling at him.

'They are the enemy. It is one way to beat them, Richard.'

'Scorched earth is hardly civilized, after all,' said Richard.

James laughed aloud. 'It worked. Look at Carthage.'

'Shall we sow salt, too? We are not the Romans. Perhaps we're sowing dragons' teeth. Did you think of that?' Willoughby shrugged. He stomped over to the can of supposedly warm water and dipped a finger in.

'Damn it,' he said, 'cold!'

Richard buckled his belt and arranged all the impedimenta about him. James opened a shutter to look out across the square.

'You know how these Boers work, Richard. They need those farms. They group there, attack from them and rest in them after their attacks. They stock up with supplies, and recover from wounds. Deny them those farms and they'll have nowhere to hide. Nowhere to run to. Have you any soap I could use? I seem to have mislaid mine.' Richard shook his head.

'Each farm we burn will make another enemy. Generations of them.'

Willoughby looked out of the window across the flat land.

'Not our concern. Do your work and say nothing.'

Richard sat on the bed. He was suddenly very tired.

'Find Saunders?' he asked and James turned for a moment and then looked away.

Richard watched the flush on James's neck. 'Of course!' James looked back at him.

'I mean it. Find the stupid man.'

'Stupid? Is that fair, James?'

Willoughby leaned on the deep sill of the window and listened to the sounds of the patrol getting ready for their march.

'He's sent up here to watch an active company. For instruction. He's bone, Richard. You know it, only you're too damn polite —'

Richard tucked the whistle and lanyard away and stood up.

'He's stubborn, priggish and inefficient,' Willoughby was going on and Richard wanted to leave, to ride in that open country and to get away from the pettiness and the jealousy and the anguish he felt here. He sighed, for James Willoughby was a good friend and he knew it.

'You'll be seeing Dorothy?

68

'You heard Slingsby.'

'Is it wise?'

'Slingsby asked me.'

'An order, James?' Richard was sarcastic. Angry. Angry because he could see the shape of things being upset. His mother would be forced to be a party to something she would find hateful.

'You don't have to, James,' he said. Willoughby looked at him for a moment and shook his head.

'Is it fair, d'you think?' Richard asked.

'It's years, Richard,' James said. He could feel, already, the pounding of his heart. He knew that he wanted to see her, to be with her and he knew it was not possible. But he had been asked by the captain and he had agreed.

'We have seen nothing of each other. Not really. One meeting — nothing. Dorothy and I have forgotten each other. I'll be a stranger.'

Richard could hear the pain in James's voice. He said gently, 'I know enough of my cousin to know that you will be no stranger.' James stared blindly from the window.

'I dare not think about it, Richard he whispered.

'You could have refused to see her.'

'Can I tell Slingsby that I was once in love with the lady?' He shook his head.

James turned and picked up the sola topee from Richard's bed. He handed it to him.

'You'd best be off,' he said and smiled. Richard stood quite still.

'To find her husband?' he asked. 'I am going to look for him, James. And to burn a few farms perhaps. Take care you don't, get burned. He may be alive yet.'

The two men were still and Richard walked out of the room. James Willoughby lay down on the bed. He could see Dorothy's dancing eyes and he could feel tears in his own.

Richard reined in, and looked back towards the small file of men he was leading.

The strength was going from the sun and the men had marched far enough. Richard waited for Sergeant Holly to reach him. He dismounted and fell into step beside Holly.

'Nearly enough, sir, for today,' said Holly and nodded at the men. They were tired. Their faces were grimy with the dust they had kicked up and sticky with sweat. So far it seemed to be a pointless business. They had seen the site of the ambush and inspected the ruin of the gun. They had nodded a respectful glance at the graves that were already looking old. Only the cairns of stones showed that soldiers were buried there.

Holly grunted as his boots struck a rock and he almost fell. Richard steadied the older, heavier man.

'Thanks, sir,' muttered Holly and stopped to get his breath. Richard stopped with him and the men marched on.

Their outriders reported no signs of Boer, indeed no sign of inhabited land at all. They had seen some buck and had tried a pot shot or two, but without luck. Richard had cursed, for fresh meat would have heartened the men and made a change from the cans of bully and tack they had with them.

Holly was pointing across the arm of the ridge.

'Over there, sir, those rocks would give us cover, sir. And the land is high enough round about for sentries.' Richard nodded.

Sergeant Holly was an experienced man, a man you could rely on. Stolid, respectable, reliable and with a knowledge of Queen's Regulations second to none. The men were afraid of him and the officers respected him. He was just the sort of man Richard had wanted with him and Slingsby had known it. Richard shook his head in wonder at the thought of Slingsby actually understanding any other human being. He seemed to be so damned cold and calculating. Richard was sure he had enjoyed hurting James Willoughby and he wasn't so sure that Slingsby didn't know that James and Dorothy had had, were having perhaps, an affair. It would be perverse, but he was a perverse man and Slingsby hated Saunders. To send an officer down-country to tell a man's wife that he might be dead, and that he was certainly missing, was very cruel, if he knew all the circumstances.

Richard tried to think who might have spoken about that particular autumn afternoon at the house in Gloucestershire. Mother didn't know, Charlotte was discreet enough and his brother — Richard was certain that Slingsby and his brother would be hardly likely to know each other.

'Very well, Sergeant Holly. Get them settled washed and watered and defensive positions. I don't want us to be caught napping by any damned Boers.'

Holly grinned and nodded and strode ahead of the advancing men. He signalled them to head for the ridge and sent a man on a pony to warn the outriders.

The darkness was absolute still and warm from the heat of the day. The men lay on their bed-rolls and watched the stars in the black sky. The moon was up and cast a blue tinge across the valley, but still the ridge and the rocks about them lay in darkness. The men tried to sleep. Sullivan and Holt sat in the shadow of a boulder and watched the night. Sullivan cupped a cigarette in his palm and dragged in the smoke. He passed the butt to Holt who took it gratefully.

'Did you notice the sergeant?' asked Sullivan quietly. Holt shook his head and let out a dribble of smoke from his lips.

'Gettin' jumpy he is, no doubt of it,' said Sullivan.

71

'Nervy like,' and Sullivan smiled into the dark and picked his teeth with the end of a match. Sullivan was afraid of no man at all, not even Holly. He had come from Cork to England and had tried many a job before joining the soldiers, which was some —' thing against his nature, for he had no liking for being ordered about by any man. But it had been necessary and him with a wife now in England. He spat into the dust and listened to the silence. There was only the occasional snicker from the lieutenant's horse, or a gentle grunt from one of the sleeping men. Sullivan stretched a little to ease his back against the boulder and he sighed.

'Like horses, Holt boyyo, waiting for the off. That's our Sergeant Holly. It's not just a damned walk we're on this time.' Holt looked at Sullivan and was surprised to hear anger in his voice.

'What d'you mean, mate?' he asked. 'It's about bloody time we got up off our arses. Months waiting in that godforsaken pig-hole of a place. Waitin', waitin' and doin' no damn thing.'

Holt was angry.

'The rest of us wants to be at something. Those bastards killed our muckers, Sullivan, don't you be forgetting it.' Sullivan shook his head at the ignorance of the man. 'You be glad we've done nothing at all. It's better nothin' than being killed. It's better nothin' than what we can be at, I'm thinking.'

'And what's that?' Holt asked. Not that he cared, except to kill a Boer or two and get his revenge, for Mallory had been a mate of his.

'Didn't you listen to Captain Slingsby? Search and burn. That's what.' Sullivan's voice hissed with bitterness and the softness of his accent became steel in his anger. 'Search and burn and dealin' wi' kids and women likely enough.'

Holt had heard the captain, but had not taken it in. He

did his job and asked no questions. Feed him and give him drink and Holt was your man.

'Dealin' with? What d'ya mean?' he asked. Sullivan looked across at him.

'Killin' is what we're paid for, isn't it?'

Holt shook his head in disbelief. 'Not women and children. Never.'

'It may be you'll be forced to it, boy. They'll be dead fierce, will those kids.'

God knows, he had been fierce against the soldiers and the police and the landowners and the rest of the English gentry and their dogs, when it was his home was threatened. When he and his da, who had the bad back, had broken the fields near the house and then had been taxed for the use of the new land, he had felt a bitter anger rising in him. He could feel, already, the stirring of something similar that he knew he had to keep down.

'They'll be dead fierce, all right, and they can shoot like the best,' he told Holt. And Holt wouldn't believe him.

'Not women. I'm not killin' no women,' he said. And he looked at Sullivan and thought he was playing with him. 'You don't mean it. It isn't the truth at all,' he said.

'That's what you may think. If you're ordered, you'll do what you're told or get stretched on the wheel, maybe. It's a shooting offence, disobeying an order, is it not? Come on, let's get our heads down.'

And Sullivan stumbled across the rock to a soft patch of moss and small fern, where he had laid his blanket and he lay down and rolled himself in the rough wool.

Smelling the bitter smell of young fern, he could see the banks of Bantry Bay with boats in the water and the house looking out across the sea, a cannon on the terrace. He thought of the patriots who had come from Bantry and from Cork and he felt sick at the thought of killing a small boy or a woman for this English Army.

73

And the sky was black that Holt watched. But he did not believe Sullivan, who had a reputation for being wild. Out on the ridge, the sentries changed and a new man watched the dawn coming across the veldt and heard a dog barking in the far distance.

8

Dorothy woke from a restless sleep and, as she had been every morning, was surprised to find that she was not at home in Cadogan Square. She was surprised to have had no greetings from Rupert and, to tell the truth, pleased by that.

She lay back and reflected that the evening before had not been so awful. They had left her alone once she had made it clear that she had no wish to be a part of the dancing. Her mind was quite made up and Rupert was now as far from her mind as she could put him. His arrogance and his jealousy she wanted no further part of, and she smiled at the thought that she was able to feel free at last.

She took the gold-framed picture of her husband from bedside table, and placed it face down. There, she thought, gesture at least and I don't care how scandalized people going to be.

Outside the sun was casting shadows through the shutters and the town was bustling with life. The early morning was the best time for the ladies to do their shopping, for gossip and for, the small things of a country town.

Dorothy smiled as she stood at the window and looked across the square. It reminded her so much of Canterbury where she had spent some time as a little girl. The drabness of the Boer women, and the presence of soldiers rather than clergymen, marked the difference between the two places. And, of course, the Gothic church was hardly to be compared with the soaring cathedral spires in the English town. But somehow, Dorothy felt content here.

She wanted so much to hear that James had come back to Pretoria. She wanted to shock people; even him.

She knew he would be worried, knew he would be afraid that they must not defy convention, knew that he would try to stop her and knew, above all, that she would win. She hugged her secret to herself; and turned before the mirror.

She was afraid that he would not come soon enough and that she would be dried up by the sun, as so many of the women out here seemed to be. She hoped it would not dry up her gaiety as it had withered theirs. She knew they had arrived, many of them, with the trekkers and that their life had been hard. They had made the choice to break the new land and to come only with God, a Bible and maybe an ox-drawn wagon. It was enough to make any woman lose heart. And to hear their ministers preaching was to hear of hellfire and brimstone and anger. Dorothy smiled as she remembered one of the Scottish officers. A Calvinist, like so many of the Boers, he felt sympathy for their beliefs, but they were fighting against the Crown and so must be put down. Men were able to make such rules and regulations and to be so unbending, she thought. They would make a misery of their lives rather than offend the mores of their club, or their family, or their regiment. Men, she reflected, are often very foolish indeed. She flicked her hair up at the back like a young girl and watched herself in the long mirror.

A gentle breeze wafted the curtains she had not bothered to draw, and Dorothy began to sing.

Mrs Gaunt and Charlotte walked slowly across the square in front of the church and went into the cool building. They knelt quietly, as they did each morning, and said a short prayer for Richard and his safety. Mrs Gaunt added one for her husband's old regiment and then she sat in the wooden pew and waited for Charlotte to finish.

When she, too, sat up Mrs Gaunt smiled at her,

patted her grey-gloved hand and they walked quietly out.

'A moment of peace,' Mrs Gaunt would say, 'is worth a thousand pounds. Well, it is to me, anyway.' And she would laugh and throw back her head so that her hat was in danger of falling off.

As they walked back to their hotel, they received the salutes of a number of officers and Mrs Gaunt observed, with amusement, the way in which Charlotte merely nodded and offered no encouragement to any of the young men.

Mrs Gaunt had a difficult daughter and she was still able to be amused by it. At least she was not seeing that red-headed Socialist. What the Colonel would have thought of him . . . Mrs Gaunt took Charlotte's hand and the two of them walked together from the church to the steps of the hotel and into the dining-room where they would eat breakfast.

'Dorothy isn't down yet,' said Charlotte and her mother looked around the room. No one they knew was down. Perhaps it was too early. The sooner Rupert came back and took Dorothy in hand, the better for all of them, Mrs Gaunt thought.

Far out in the veldt, a bird circled, halted and swooped to the ground. Under the soft, black cloth of his jacket, the man had bled slowly to death and the bird was first at the kill. It began to peck and snap at the dead man.

9

Truus Meyer gutted the chicken, floured it, browned it and threw it into the pot. A few vegetables and some meal she and Piet would be fed for the next two days. She wanted to think and cooking distracted her. Quickly, she threw the guts on the low fire and strode outside with the peelings from the vegetables for the scrabbling chickens.

She leaned back against the post, holding the veranda rail and closed her eyes. She had felt no pain since that time, two days ago. It had frightened her and still she had no idea what it could be.

She knew that the soldier would recover now. He had stopped sweating and was asking for drinks. Some broth from the chicken would give him strength. Her lips tightened and she tried to put the soldier from her mind. Hadn't he come here, ready to die, and hadn't she mended him? His ways were not her ways, but he was made by God and she found it hard to hate him. Hadn't Jan said the same when he lay in the bed with her on his last night?

'He is a strong man, Truus. He was badly hurt and he lived for the journey. It was not possible and yet he did live.'

She had not wanted to talk about him, but there he was. It seemed that he was a message, maybe, and she was not sure she wanted to listen to his word. Like those uncomfortable prophets in the wilderness.

He lay and said little and he watched her whenever she walked into his small room. He wanted to live. She knew that. He had the will to live. He must have something to go back to, something to hold on to, something important. Truus shook her head and looked up at the blinding sun.

They had been here now for twelve years. Piet had been born the first year. Together they had broken the land, built the house, bought cattle, chickens, raised the herd and the corn. They had fought others to keep them off their land and it had been fruitful. There was water for the whole year, even in the bad times and they were lucky. Jan was good with the land and loved it. Each year they had made a celebration of the day they had stopped from the column of trekkers and said this was as far as they would go.

Neither of them had spoken. They had stopped by the trees and watched as the rest of the column wound on in the dust to the north. And when the predicant had come back to them to ask what was the matter, they had looked at each other and then at him and Jan pointed to the earth and said, 'I will stand here, now. My wife and I will stay,' and the predicant had been angry, for the agreement was that they should all go as far as he said. But he could do nothing and rode away without blessing the land.

Truus pushed a strand of hair back and shut her eyes again. There was no need for his blessing, she thought. It had been a hard winter and they had built a small room to live in, against the wind and the rain. They had to plant enough to live the next spring. Truus remembered that she had felt so tired with Piet in her. But they worked on and it had been good. Truus was surprised to find tears in her eyes.

Across the veldt, shadows began to move. By the side of a huge ant-hill, a mass of feathers jerked and tugged as the sun went down. The vultures were already perched in the sagging trees beside the waterhole. They had eaten too much and they watched the small birds digging and prying with sharp, snapping beaks into the bloody mess that lay under their claws.

The black jacket was in tatters and the shirt had been

ripped and shredded in the impatient struggle. Quite suddenly, the sun dipped and the veldt was dark. The birds rose into the air, gorged. In the ant-hill, a million, million blind creatures whirled and turned. Beside the hill, blood dried into the warm earth. It was still.

10

Sullivan ran, laughing, from the chicken coop with three birds. They were squawking with fear and feathers were flying as the soldier raced towards the sergeant.

'Sullivan,' roared Sergeant Holly, 'put those bloody chickens down.'

'Oh, come on, Sergeant. Sure they'd make the most wonderful supper. Think of them on a fire now and brown and crisp and sweet.' Sergeant Holly looked around the little yard of the farm they were searching and then nodded.

'Two will do, Sullivan, Two only.'

Sullivan grinned and dropped one of the birds, which scuttered off in a cloud of feathers. A soldier aimed a kick at the bird and the men laughed.

'Number one section!' Holly roared and the rest of the men stopped probing in the hay with bayonets, and kicking in the water butts, breaking up chicken coops and dog kennels in case a Boer was hiding. They straggled over to Sergeant Holly.

'Look lively, damn your eyes,' he shouted and they fell in quickly. Another useless search. No sign of any commando. Only an old woman and her without a single word of English. She had said nothing to them. Lieutenant Gaunt had tried to explain to her, in halting Dutch, what they wanted. She had just turned away from him and walked into the house.

Sullivan walked over with the two birds hanging limp in his hands. He held them up for the men to see and there was a ragged cheer.

Richard Gaunt stepped from the house on to the veranda step. He was wiping his jacket with a handkerchief as the Sergeant stepped smartly up to him.

The door slammed behind the lieutenant. The men whirled round, expecting firing. Richard hadn't moved. He was staring at the handkerchief.

'Nothing, sir,' reported Holly. Richard threw the handkerchief to the ground.

'Inside, sir?' asked Holly. Richard shook his head.

'Nothing. An old woman. She said nothing.'

Holly shrugged. 'No sir. I suppose not sir. Seeing what we're doing.'

'She spat on me, Sergeant,' said Richard. 'She spat on me.'

Sergeant Holly nodded. 'Yes, sir.' He looked at the young soldier. 'Can we carry on now, sir?'

Richard slowly unbuttoned his jacket and took it off. The men watched, surprised, as he draped it across the saddle of the horse.

'Yes, Sergeant. Yes. Carry on. We've done all we can here.'

Inside the house the old woman tugged the curtains back and watched as the column of English led by the young man on the horse walked slowly away. Her lined face was impassive and only the hatred in her eyes showed that she was moved in any way by them.

Richard rode slowly beside the column of men and did not speak. He was wrapped in his own thoughts as they approached the last farm on the map. After a night there, they would return to Headquarters and report failure.

They had already turned over six places. At each they had found no resistance and had seen neither men nor any sign of Boer troops using the places. Each time, though, they had met with silence from the women and an absolute refusal to talk. At one farm, a woman had called away her children because these are 'rooineks and have guns to kill your fathers with.'

Richard had never seen such hatred and such anger

and it frightened him much more than the thought of bullets or bayonets. Bringing the war to the women and the children was sickening for him and he knew it sickened the men also. They were sullen and angry and it would take only a word or two for them all to show their anger. After all, weren't many of the soldiers from farms as poor as the ones they were searching and brutalizing? It was an order, he knew, and perhaps it was a necessary one, but Richard could not believe it. And to be spat on by an old lady – he felt degraded by the work, unclean.

Across the dark earth was Rietsplaas, where they would rest for the night. And then they would rendezvous with Captain Slingsby and his squad back at the river crossing.

Below the warming earth, the blind ants sensed the blood near the surface and began to scrabble towards it. Some ran out from the hill and found the shreds of cloth and flesh on the earth and began to drag them back into the mound of earth to feed on. The mouth of the man was open in the stuf rictus smile and his sockets were empty. In the gristle behind them, two ants met, touched and passed by, into the bone. It would be a long, hot day but they were blind and unfeeling.

11

In Rietsplaas, Saunders opened his eyes and looked at the light streaming in through the small, high window. The chicken soup he had taken last night seemed to have given strength to his limbs and he smiled. At last he could begin to think. A small movement by the door startled him and he strained to turn his head to see what had caused it.

Looking at him from the doorway, he saw the dark eyes of the little boy who was whittling white shaves of wood from a long stick. The shavings lay on the floor at his feet as he watched Saunders.

Saunders lay back and called: 'Mevrou, Mevrou . . .' Truus came and looked down at him.

'Piet,' she said, 'lets om te drink vir Captain Saunders,' but the boy looked at her, shook his head and went out of the house. Truus was angry and went after him, but he had run to the barn and she did not bother to follow. She picked up a cup and took the captain a drink. Saunders was smiling.

'He'd cut my throat sooner, Mevrou,' he said and lay back on the bed.

He knew how much the boy hated him and he thought he knew why. Indeed, he admired the spirit of the boy as much as he had contempt for this creature who had looked after him. She was well enough to look on. A peasant woman and simple, he supposed.

'He is a good boy,' Truus defended her son.

Saunders was surprised by her English which she spoke well. She was proud of having been to school as a child. She had learned it there.

Truus sighed. 'He is a good boy, but he needs his father now. He wishes to go to the fighting.' Saunders was surprised.

'He can't fight grown men. A child — the English soldier — the finest —' She laughed at him.

'My Piet shoots better than my man. That's the truth. So, he will shoot better than any English. Piet will go, if the Lord wishes.' Truus wiped her hands on her apron and stood in the doorway.

Behind her, the light streamed in. Her hair was golden and she had a fine, strong body. So different from Dorothy, who seemed to be so fragile, delicate. Saunders smiled ruefully, for he knew her to be as strong as this woman before him appeared to be.

'Our men first and then our children – "Your hands are defiled with blood, and your fingers with iniquity, your lips have spoken lies. The way of peace you know not." He is like his father. He will go.' Truus turned away into the main room so that this soldier should not see her tears.

She was afraid, but she did not know why. She walked to the scrubbed table and sat in the big chair with the long arms that Jan, her husband, used. Before her, on the table, was the Bible, his Bible and his son's Bible. She began to read aloud in Dutch and through the open door Saunders could hear her.

> *Hy lei die gevangene uit in voorspoed:*
> *Oh God, toe U uitgetrek het voor U volk,*
> *Toe U voorgestap het in die Wildernis, Sela:*
> *Het die aarde gebewe*

Piet stood in the doorway listening to his mother as she read the book slowly. His face was tired and drawn. He watched his mother as she closed the book. He listened as Saunders spoke from his bed hi the back room.

' "He bringeth out those which are bound with chains —" It is a strong psalm, Mevrou Meyer.'

Truus did not move. Her head rested on her hands, the long hair falling to cover her face and Piet couldn't see the tears on her face.

'You understand well, Captain. It is strong. "Let God arise, let his enemies be scattered. As smoke is driven away, so drive them away." We pray that each night, Captain. I'm sorry.'

Piet walked out of the house in disgust. He could understand nothing that was being said and he wanted no part of it. He wanted to ride away into the veldt to join his father.

Truus went back into the room where Saunders lay.

'Your pain, Captain?' she asked.

'Nearly gone. Thank you.'

Truus filled the oil lamp from the small store of oil and trimmed the wick.

'You were lucky,' she said, and cut the wick lower.

'Lucky not to be shot out of hand; lucky my damned horse was shot, or lucky to end up alive, here?'

She smiled at the bitterness in his voice. It was something she understood. He had been hurt more by the loss of his pride than by the shot in his shoulder.

'I was lucky to be brought here,' he agreed. Truus stood by the window and opened the shutters. Dust danced in the sunlight.

'I think it is harder for us than for the men, truly. They ride and hunt and — my man is a good farmer, Captain. It is what he wants. The land is heavy and we have fine crops each year. But now — it is very hard for a woman. Piet will go soon. He will join his father perhaps. You thought him a kind man?'

Saunders looked at her in surprise. He didn't understand.

'My man. Didn't you know, Captain Saunders? That man who was leading the commando. He is my man. He is a kind man. Truly gentle.' Truus felt the need to explain why her man had brought back a prisoner. He could so easily have left him in the veldt to die.

'I miss him. They do say that some people are so close they feel what another feels. When I was bearing Piet, Jan had pains in his belly. My pain he felt. It's the truth. He was weak from the pain.'

And, quite suddenly, Truus knew what the pain had been that she felt under the tree by the edge of the field. She knew that the shocking agony had been more than something in her. She felt the tears start again and run down her cheeks as she spoke. She was glad that the Captain was too weak to look back at her, as she stood by the window.

'You will find it hard, here, Captain, to understand. We came here, broke the land together, built this home together. On the post of that door we carved our names. He is away now and I see him — never.'

Truus Meyer walked out of the house and sat in the rocking-chair by the stoep, buried her face in her hands and cried silently.

12

James Willoughby trotted up Church Street and noticed nothing of the bustle. He had too much on his mind to care that a team driver swore fluently, and for a long time, as he halted his oxen for the lieutenant to pass. He noticed nothing of the Afrikaaner who stood and watched him pass, and who ached for the chance of a rifle and one round. He saw nothing of the beautiful square in front of the church, as he rode to the hotel in which he knew that Dorothy Saunders was staying. He dismounted, handed the reins of the horse to a black and stepped stiffly up the step. He walked into the relative darkness of the hotel. A few men looked up from their seats in the lounge. Across the lobby, Willoughby might have seen the door of the billiard room. But he did not look.

At the desk there was no one. He had screwed himself up to this moment and now he could feel his heart fluttering and his stomach cramped like a boy. He could feel the backs of his legs stiffen in apprehension and he licked his dry lips. It was stupid to be so afraid of meeting a woman. It was cowardly of him to shirk his duty. He looked helplessly about the room and still no one came to the desk.

He could hear the distinct sound of laughter and the hurried trip of a lady's shoes. At the head of the curved stairs stood Charlotte Gaunt and Mrs Gaunt, ready to go to the hospital.

James Willoughby turned away too slowly to avoid recognition, and Mrs Gaunt hurried down the stairs to stop him leaving.

'I do declare, Mr Willoughby, that you were evading us,' she said. 'Is there any reason? Richard isn't —' She was suddenly afraid and only reassured when he shook his head.

'I left Richard in fine fettle,' he said. 'He sends his, his love.' The word stuck in his throat.

'And you, Lieutenant?' asked Charlotte, 'here in Pretoria. May we know why?'

James wanted to leave now. Dorothy might find him here and he knew that if she did, then his opportunity would be lost. He looked at the door.

'If it's a secret, then, of course, we don't wish you to tell,' said Charlotte and smiled at him. 'You don't have to look so furtive, though, James. Do you?'

He smiled at her and shook his head. A black boy opened the doors and a breath of hot sir puffed across the lobby. The door shut again.

'No secret,' he said. 'I am here to report to Headquarters and to rejoin A Company. I, well, I do have other business.' He hesitated to talk about it and Mrs Gaunt said nothing.

'Have you any news of Rupert Saunders?' Charlotte asked, even though her mother tried to stop her. James shook his head.

I'd rather not talk of that. Not until I have talked with Mrs Saunders. It isn't too promising, that's all.' The two ladies were frightened by what he told them.

'I assure you, ladies, that many men have been in much worse situations. And should he be a prisoner, then the war is over for him and he is safe enough.'

James did not want to believe that, and yet he knew that this was the chance. He did not want to hope that Saunders was dead and yet he couldn't help hoping it. He walked with Mrs Gaunt to the door of the hotel.

'Are you sure it is wise, Mr Willoughby?' she asked, 'to see Dorothy?'

He shook his head and smiled at her.

'I have been asked to, Mrs Gaunt. Ordered to see her.' She paused on the top step and looked not at him, but at the church across the square.

'There are some, Mr Willoughby, who believe that their duty is to be faithful, true, honest. You understand me, I think.'

'There are some, Mrs Gaunt, who give up hope, who believe that happiness is not possible, who waste their lives. I am not one of those. Not any more. Not after what I have seen in this war. I beg your pardon ma'am,' he said, walking away from her across to the trees and beyond them round the corner of the carpet store. He had been afraid and had run away from the meeting he knew he must have.

RIETSPLAAS

1

Sullivan, Macarthy and Carvey raced across the open ground between the huge tree and the farm buildings up to the step and through into the main room, rifles at the ready and wanting to shoot. They faced Truus Meyer who sat at the table with a Bible open. She continued to read from it and not one of the soldiers would have known that she had hurriedly opened it when Piet ran in, shouting that the soldiers were coming.

'*Gaan na jou kamer, asseblief*, Piet,' she had ordered and he had gone to his room. She had opened the book and now sat reading aloud.

'*Hy was verdruk en verdruktes, en tog hy het sy mond nie oopmaak nie, hy is soos 'n lam na die slagplek gelei word, en soos 'n skaap voor sy skeerders is stil, sodat hy nie sy mond oopmaak..*'

Sullivan and the others felt foolish, standing looking at this woman, who read without glancing up and without faltering. Sullivan motioned to the others and he went out to find the Lieutenant and Sergeant Holly.

The other two men ordered the woman out. She rose and walked out slowly. Holly pushed her with the butt of his rifle as she emerged from the house.

'Over there, lady, against the rail. Double quick, imshi. Come on, face front, hands on the rail!' he shouted at her and she did as she was told. Sullivan had gone back into the house.

Suddenly there was a shout and the sounds of a scuffle in the house. Sullivan came out carrying the kicking, biting Piet under one arm.

'Sullivan!' shouted Holly and Sullivan threw the boy onto the boards at his feet. The boy was up and back at him in an instant and Sullivan blocked the punches and kicks of the lad. Lieutenant Gaunt ran over and Holly grabbed the boy and handed him to his mother.

'What the devil are you doing, Sullivan? That boy is near enough a baby.' Richard was angry.

'Never the doubt of it, sir, and him with teeth like needles and boots like rifle butts, sir. Aren't I bruised from head to toe with him?'

Richard turned to Truus who was calming the boy.

'*Mevrou, se vir die kerel —*'

'I was at my prayers, mister,' she said in English. Richard was surprised.

'I'm sorry. But we have a job to do.'

'You wish to search?' Richard nodded.

'And my men will stay the night. They will use your barn.'

'I see.' Truus was quite calm now.

'Nothing will be harmed, I promise that, Mevrou.' She shook her head.

'Unless you find my man under my bed. Or rifles in the roof?'

Richard shrugged.

'We have our orders.'

'Orders!' she scoffed. 'Yes, I have already heard what you have done. You, someone like you. I have friends and they told us. The only things that feast now on their land are the vultures. Homes burned to the ground — They said it. I didn't believe men could do such things.'

Richard turned to the sergeant. He did not want the men to hear her.

'Carry on, Sergeant. The barn. Sullivan will watch this door.' He turned back to Truus, 'Mevrou, you speak English well.' She looked at him.

'I understand well enough. Now, I never speak it unless it is necessary. "He was brought as a lamb to the slaughter and as a sheep before his shearers is dumb"' She turned and walked into the house.

Holly looked at Richard's surprised face and for the first time for a week, he laughed. Richard rounded on him.

'Sa'rnt! Get on!' And Richard strode after this strange woman and into the house. She was sitting at the table again and Sullivan was at the door watching. Piet was standing by the fireplace, sulking.

Richard walked over to the table and looked down at Truus and she looked back up at him. Richard looked away and took in the room. It was bigger and better furnished than the other farms had been. It seemed comfortable and well cared for and some of the pieces of furniture had obviously been brought from the old country.

She watched this young man looking at her home, and waited.

'Mevrou, will you give me your word that there are no Boer rebels here?' he asked.

'My son is a Boer, mister.'

'Men, Mevrou. Don't waste my time, please.'

'No other Boer men.'

'And none use this place?'

She looked at the light coming in through the open door. She could hear the soldiers searching and breaking down doors outside.

'Well?' the young officer asked.

'How many have you asked this question?' she said.

'About eight women.'

'And they said?'

'They all said no,' said Richard. She sighed and shook her head.

'We are a God-fearing people, Lieutenant. But we

93

love our men.' He was aware that she was making him feel awkward. It 1 irritated him.

'You haven't answered my question.' And she smiled up at him and, for the first time, he saw that she was a very beautiful woman.

'I have,' she said. 'I have.'

Richard, baffled, turned away from the woman towards Sullivan.

'Look out, sir!' shouted Sullivan and levelled his rifle. Richard turned fast and there, propped in the doorway with a bandage across his chest and around his shoulder, stood Rupert Saunders.

'Gaunt,' he said, 'delighted to see you.'

Truus Meyer watched the two men and behind her eyes she was quite dead. Piet did not move and they knew it was all over.

A bloated blue fly crawled along the sinus of the dead man and through the socket where his eye had been. It deliberated a moment on the raw rim of the eye and then stepped down into the flayed meat where the cheek had been. Already the flesh was rotting and already this fly had laid its eggs under the carapace that covered the soft white lobes of the brain. The smell lay low and heavy on the ground in the afternoon sun and the heat had begun to melt the flesh to a rotten brown pulp. The fat fly wrenched itself out of the sticky face and flew away.

The two men ate soup and chicken and were now drinking tea. Behind them, Truus stirred the pot and listened to their conversation. She got the impression that neither of these men liked the other.

He was a young man, this lieutenant with the fair hair and the blue eyes, and she thought he looked a fine enough sort of a man. Truus straightened up and took the plates from the table. The young man thanked her and she ignored him. She heard the captain laugh and she knew he despised her. She wished for a moment that she had let him die, or that she had left him alone for long enough with Piet, her little boy. He would have done what he did with the pigs and slit the throat of this *rooinek* who laughed at her.

She hated now, like her son hated. She hated because she knew enough to know what her pain had been and because this man thought her weak. Well, he would soon know.

Saunders sat back and looked at Richard. Little bloody prig, he thought, as he watched Richard drinking his tea. Anyone'd think he was at the vicarage tea party, instead of in a Boer slut's cabin. He looked back at the woman standing by the fire and he laughed. She was a fine-looking woman, and good, perhaps, for a man's bed once in a while, if he wasn't too fastidious, but to be married to her — God knows she'd be wild and dirty, like they all were. Damn lucky he hadn't died of gangrene.

'You're not married, Gaunt?' He knew very well that Richard was not married and it amused him. Richard liked Dorothy above all his relations and Saunders knew, also, that he disliked Rupert Saunders, Captain in the Cotswolds, almost as much.

'You're not married?' he asked again and Richard stopped staring at the table and looked up at his brother officer.

Richard disliked both the man and his manners. He disliked his arrogance and his damned certainty that he was in the right. He hated his indifference to the situation that he, Richard, was placed in by the discovery of an officer in this house.

Richard thanked the Boer woman for her hospitality and for her generosity in allowing him to take food at her table. He knew she could not refuse, but she could have done it with a far worse grace. He did not know that she felt sorry for him.

His men were safely quartered outside and tomorrow, at first light, they would trek out and back down to the Kraasche river crossing to the meeting with Slingsby. Before that, he knew that he had to make a decision about this farm, about this woman, the child and even about himself.

'You're not married, Gaunt?' Saunders asked. Richard looked up from the table.

'Hardly. Subalterns don't.'

Saunders poured another cup.

'It is a singular institution, don't you know? Woman loses her freedom, so to speak, and gains roots, respectability, security. And a man loses his freedom, but owns an asset, one could say.'

Behind them, Truus Meyer listened.

'"Owns", Captain?' He didn't even turn round to answer her.

'Yes. "Owns", Mevrou.'

'We have different ways here, Captain, I think.' Saunders turned now and he sneered as he spoke.

'No doubt. You still read the Good Book.'

'We believe it, yes.' Richard got up from the table and walked out.

'I'll see my men now. Thank you, Mevrou.' Truus stood at the doorway and watched him go across to the barn. She could hear the sounds of a mouth organ playing. It sounded very lonely.

'D'you ever, mister, d'you ever have black doubts in the back of your mind? Black fears?' She didn't turn back into the room. 'Never. Why?' said Saunders.

'I do. And I pray to God. That is our strength Mister. You have your wife.' She was crying now and she leaned her head against the cool wood of the door. Her hands twisted the rough apron she wore. Saunders watched her without moving.

96

'Of course I have. You heard me —' he said. Truus stared out into the dark night.

'You don't speak of her. Ever.' Saunders grinned. No damn business of this woman if he did or not.

'Dorothy's a fine woman. Well educated. Well bred. Knows what's what. You wouldn't understand.' He swirled the leaves in the bottom of the china cup. 'I would not trust myself, though. In any woman's hands.' Truus turned and stared at him.

'Thank you,' she said and walked slowly to the back of the room. He shrugged. He had hurt her feelings.

'I didn't mean — I beg your pardon.' After all, she had fed him and cleaned his wound.

Truus stood at the end of the table with a cloth and began to wipe it clean.

'It is not my concern, Captain. You will go tomorrow. I shall be more than pleased. To think as you do. To think you own a woman. You are an arrogant man, Captain. You think I nursed you because I wanted you to live?'

He looked up sharply. Surely this was the reason. This weakness was something he despised in her. 'It was your duty,' he said. 'As a Christian.' She laughed then. And she was close to him as she leaned on the scrubbed top of the table.

'We have forgotten Christ, I think. With this war we pray to another God. But he is hidden from us. I nursed you because you would make a useful prisoner. You are an English Officer and a valuable man for trading. That is why we wanted you alive. No Boer woman wants any of you alive with her man away from her. Away from their land.'

Saunders looked up at her and saw the hatred in her eyes and the anger that made her shake as she leaned on the table. She was crying now and they were tears of rage.

'D'you know what this land means to us? I love the land more than any single thing, save my man and my son. If the minister said to me, choose between God and your land, I know which I would choose; and why Jan, my husband, would choose the land also. You would take Rietsplaas, you would take it from us and I would wish you to die, Captain. My little boy, Piet, he wanted to kill you. Each night, when you were delirious he asked me and each time I said no. But only because we could trade you. You are cattle, mister. No more to me than that.'

She stood at the end of the table, exhausted. He was hunched in his chair, completely shaken by her attack and by the understanding that she had given him. She had degraded him by saving him. She had made him no better than barter goods. Well, she should be paid for that. Indeed she should. He looked up at her and his face was white with anger, his lips in a tight line and the eyes screwed up with bitterness.

Truus walked out of the room and across the yard to the tree on the edge of the first field. It was quite dark outside.

2

Dorothy stood near the mirror. Her long, golden dress caught the light as James looked at her. She turned away and he saw, the white of her slender neck and the softness of the skin. He had told her about Rupert and she had said nothing. For a long, long time they stood quite silent. The dim light in the room only emphasized the tension.

'I am sorry,' he said. 'It was such a confusion, Dorothy, I can't be sure of anything.'

'You think he may have been killed?' It was utterly calm. A statement more than a question. He nodded. She turned back towards him now and sat at the piano, which stood in the corner of the lounge.

'D'you know, James, I've hardly seen my husband? Oh, I'm bidden to regimental shows or to functions at the War Office. I'm decoration, I suppose. It's all been a bit of a waste, really.' She looked up and smiled softly at him. Her huge eyes in the white, strained face looked at him now, for the first time. He's embarrassed, she thought, and I mustn't make a scene. Poor James. How difficult it must have been and nothing's changed between us. But to say it, to do something about it, to accomplish the vows made, now that they were face to face again. 'Dorothy, d'you think you ought to tell me —' 'For heaven's sake, if I can't tell you the truth, James, who can I tell it to?' she flashed with anger. He knew she was right. She smiled at him and rose from the seat and controlled her anger.

'Richard Gaunt's mother is here. You know? And Charlotte. You remember? We tried to marry you off to her one autumn.'

He remembered the autumn. In Gloucestershire. He remembered the little girl, Charlotte, and he remembered

99

Dorothy then as she knew he would.

'Yes,' he said, 'I thought time would have changed — I never thought that we'd see each other again.'

She walked slowly away from him towards the window. She looked out for a moment into the square and it seemed to be a thousand miles away from them, in this room.

'It's all a little foolish James, isn't it? You come out here to fight a stupid, squalid little war. You turn down all the best things — I don't want to cry, James.'

He stood a moment and then turned and walked to the door. She cried without touching her face. The tears just ran down.

'James,' she said and he stopped. 'I'll stop. I — I won't make a scene.' She wiped her eyes with the back of her hand like a little girl.

'Richard was right. He warned me. He tried to stop me coming. For very much the best of reasons, my dear. People talk —'

'Do they concern you?' Dorothy knew now that one battle was over and another about to be won. He shook his head and she smiled through her tear-filled eyes. She held out her hand to him.

'I've already forgotten the time, my dear. I don't care any more what anyone says. It doesn't matter does it?' He looked into her eyes and took her hand.

'You must think, my dear. You will be cut off. Society will certainly turn its back on you.'

She giggled suddenly, like a child.

'Fiddlesticks to society. I feel like a little girl, James, I don't even feel guilty. Should I?'

James shook his head. It would be hard for them both, he knew that.

'I shall have to resign,' he said.

'But you've worked so hard,' she protested. He had worked hard and to throw it away like this, he suddenly realized, didn't' matter.

'I've spent five years of my life, Dorothy. Wasted them. We both have.' They laughed together.

'Poor Rupert, he never understood anything,' she said. And like a douche of cold water, James came back to reality.

'Dorothy, he may still be alive. I want you to promise me something. I want you to promise me that you will not make a decision yet. I want you to think —' She put a finger on his lips and shook her head.

'I made up my mind long ago, James. I need no time to think. We have to plan for something different. A different life. Perhaps here.' She held his arms with strong, white hands and he laughed at the determination in her face. 'Why not? We could stay. The war will be won. It's a fine country. Why don't we?'

James leaned down to her eager face and kissed her. Outside, a man shrieked at a team of oxen. Around them, in the hotel, would be a depth of disapproval they would have to face, but now he held this woman and they loved each other.

It was the evening of the third day and already the lump on the veldt was unrecognizable as a man. The limbs were jumbled. There were gaping rents his the pelvis and abdomen. Splinters of new bone lay about, where the dogs had chewed on the carrion. The eggs up in the soft lobes of the brain were warmed and safe. At a distance from the body lay a bandoleer of bullets and a shapeless black hat that, perhaps, a woman had made, one summer. The purple organs above the bowels glistened in the last light of the day.

3

Richard knew that he had to make a decision. He knew, now, that Saunders had been brought here. He knew that a Boer Commando had been through the farm. He did not want to admit it.

Saunders was in bed, tired from the unaccustomed exercise of the day. He would have a hard few days on the journey to the crossing.

Richard sat at the table in the room, alone. Truus Meyer sat in her rocking-chair, which he could hear creaking softly. She had been weeping. Her little boy sat on the step and shaved a stick with the knife. Richard had tried to speak with him, but the boy had glared and spat on the dusty ground and walked away.

Truus Meyer shook her head at Richard.

'He doesn't know English,' she said. 'You knew that.' Richard walked into the house, unwelcome.

He could hear the mournful sound of the mouth organ in the barn. For the first time he held someone's whole life in his hands and he could dispose of it as he wished. It was something he was born to and he knew that he could not fail, but nevertheless he knew, also, that he would always remember the look in the eyes of the Boer boy.

Richard walked into the room where Saunders lay reading. He closed the door quietly and Saunders looked across at him.

'All well?' he asked. Richard nodded. It was all well outside. Holly had placed sentries and the men would soon be bedding down.

'Get some sleep then, man. Take my advice. The men are settled, fed and watered so to speak.' Saunders pulled at his pipe and turned the page. Richard sat at the end of the bed.

'I want you to answer me a question. Will you?' Saunders looked at him.

'Yes. Of course. If I can.' Richard looked so damnably serious. He took everything so seriously.

'Please think carefully before you answer me.' He paused and Saunders laid the book down. 'How did you get here from the river crossing?'

Saunders smiled at the transparent concern that Richard was showing. Richard knew how and he knew what his answer would be.

'I was brought here.'

'By whom?'

Saunders shook his head. 'You know who.'

Richard stood and moved away from the bed. He ran his hand along the smooth back of a chair near the window. He, listened to the night sounds outside this peaceful and beautiful place. He did not turn round.

'Not by a woman, a child, not by chance, not by a stray horse?' Saunders remembered what Truus Meyer had said to him and his mouth tightened into a thin and angry line.

'The truth is Gaunt, that I was brought here by her husband. I was brought here by his commando which came through for fresh supplies and horses. I was to be exchanged. Used later.' He would pay that bitch of a peasant back.

Richard turned to him now and Saunders saw how hurt Richard was. He smiled. Richard walked to the door and unlatched it.

'You had only to lie Rupert, didn't you?' Saunders lay back in the bed and smiled at him and shook his head in amazement.

'Lie? Why? I owe them nothing. You heard me. I was to be exchanged. I was coin. Barter. Nothing else.' Richard stood quite still.

'She saved your life,' he said.

'All the better to exchange me with. I was no use to them dead, after all.' Richard was surprised at the bitterness and the anger in Saunders.

'You don't care?' Saunders shrugged and picked up his book.

'No. Why should I?'

Richard unlatched the door angrily. 'If you don't know why — I hope you can sleep!'

He slammed the door as he left Saunders smiling to himself. The captain carefully turned the page of his book. He would be barter for no woman.

Sullivan sat on the hay in one of the stalls used for the horses. He looked down at the men who sat on the floor in front of him. In the corner of the barn, Williams played the mouth organ softly and the dim yellow light of the lamps cast dark shadows beyond the sleeping forms of some of the men. Bits of equipment were draped over the beams and lay in small piles on the floor near the blankets of each man.

Sergeant Holly stood at the dark doorway and watched as Sullivan spoke to the others.

'In a pig's ear. In a pig's ear!' he hissed. 'If this is soldierin' yer fit for nothin' but women's work.' Holly stepped angrily towards the Irishman.

'Shut your mouth, Sullivan.' Sullivan turned to look at Holly and smiled at him. Holly stood his ground.

'You'd not be telling me to me face Sergeant, that this is the work you joined the Army for? Now is it? Will we burn this farm, or will we not? You know damn fine a man such as meself could as easy slip off and do men's work with the Irish Regiment, on the Boer side, as do this work of harassing women.'

'Desertion, Sullivan?'

'Sweet Jesus don't I know that! It's better'n holding little strips of boys and ripping down homes for a trace of the Boer. To burn the place down after.'

'Orders,' said Holly and turned on the group who sat at Sullivan's feet. 'And you'd do well to remember it.'

Sullivan laughed and shook his head and lay back on the straw. Holly waited a moment and then strode out of the barn. A man such as Sullivan could be dangerous at a time like this. Holly knew that Lieutenant Gaunt was having a bad time trying to make the decision to burn the place. But burned it would have to be, if the Boer had used it. And with the captain left there was proof enough, surely.

The sergeant looked across at the house and saw the woman rocking slowly in her chair on the step. He lit a cigarette and waited in the shadow of the barn. He had work he had to do and he would do it. But he waited for the officers to make up their minds, because that was what they were here for. He would do what he was ordered, no questions and double quick.

Truus Meyer went into the house. She came out with a small bag and the boy's shirt. She began to sew the shirt in the light that spilled from the room. Sergeant Holly strolled across the yard and out to check the picket line beyond the big tree. Truus Meyer did not turn her head to watch the sergeant, but she saw him nevertheless.

At the tree, the sergeant stopped. Richard Gaunt stood looking out over the dark land.

'It's all quiet, sir.'

Richard nodded. He did not look at the sergeant. He had been wrestling with the situation. He admired the woman and he knew that whatever he did would be wrong.

'Sentries have been relieved, sir. It's all quiet.'

'More than can be said for the men, Sergeant. They should be getting some sleep. We've a hard day ahead of us.' Sergeant Holly adjusted the choking collar he wore.

'I was wondering sir, would you mind. I'm a bit

bothered; like. I wonder if you'd be good enough to step over later, sir? To the men's quarters, sir.'

'Why?' Richard turned sharply on Holly.

'Well, sir, there's a few as feel we're not soldierin' sir. Dealin' wi' women and kids. There's some don't like it, sir.' Holly stood straight. He'd done all he had to do. It was up the lieutenant now.

'They'll do as they are ordered, Sergeant.' Holly step; back.

'They will, sir. It's only two, three of them. No more like. It's a good section, sir. You know that.'

'Very well, Sergeant. Thank you, Sergeant.' Holly walked away smartly and left Richard staring towards the dim lights in the dark veldt.

A good farm, he knew, and one torn with great labour from the land. He walked slowly across to the house and stood watching the woman sewing in the near darkness. She did not look at him when she spoke.

' "The mighty men of Babylon have forborne to fight; their might is failed; they become as women; they have burned her dwelling places — the men of war are affrightened".'

She sighed and pushed away her hair from her eyes. She rocked back in the chair and now she looked at the young man watching her. She could not hate him. He was too young, too fresh. As her man had been before they broke the land. She could not hate him. Not yet.

Richard walked into the barn and looked about. Through the swirls of pipe smoke, and the hazy glow from the few lamps still left alight, he saw a group of men around Sullivan. Sergeant Holly stood nearby.

'I'd be a bloody pauper for guts, if I had this work to do each day.' Sullivan's rich voice carried to where Richard stood in the shadows. His thin face and cropped hair gave the man a satanic look in the flickering light. The paleness was strange, when all the rest of the men had reddened under the furious sun they had experienced on the veldt.

'I'd tell you all a story,' he went on.

'You'd do better to hold your tongue,' ordered the sergeant as Richard stepped into the light.

'Let him tell his story, Sergeant. Sit down.' The men sat. Sullivan still stood and seemed reluctant to go on with his tale.

'Well, Sullivan? You like the sound of your voice. Let's hear the story.'

Sullivan saw the young Englishman and remembered the times he had seen Englishmen, very like this one, who had cowed his people and made them eat dirt.

'I'd rather we forgot the whole thing, sir.' He felt awkward talking to this officer and it made him angry that he should feel so intimidated.

'Sure it might harm me, sir.' The lieutenant waited and Sullivan noticed how tired he looked.

'You'll remember sir, what I am, sir? When I tell it.'

'What are you, Sullivan?'

'A man, sir.' Sullivan was looking straight into the lieutenant's eyes and the simple statement was a challenge. The men stirred and watched the officer.

'I'll remember, Sullivan,' he said and watched as Sullivan sat on an upturned barrel. The men craned closer and Sergeant Holly spat in disgust.

Sullivan looked around the men but he could no longer see them. He watched as Williams still played softly in the corner of the barn but he heard no sound.

In his ears was the roaring of a winter sea and he could suddenly feel the dull ache in his back and the numb rawness of his hands from the oars he had pulled. And to tell these men the story was an effort of great will, for he had harboured, deep inside, a burning anger against all such as these in their English uniforms and to be one now, himself, was an irony he did not wish to be reminded of. Wouldn't his father have cursed him to his grave, and his mother too?

'I was born in a little place. Crookhaven is a small mess of cottages on the edge of the water. There is a harbour as soft as down. There it is always a grand day, a soft day d'you see and the people very gentle. To be an Irishman, d'you see, is to be something else too.'

Sullivan searched for the words. He saw the nodding heads of the shawled old women at the cottage doors and the dogs lying in the dirt beside them. Their hands were busy with the knitting and the sewing. Under the smoke-filled turf of the roofs, the sails and the oars of the boats were stored. He could hear the soft lap of the water and the sound of gulls screaming over the fish guts on the shore.

'When I was a boy, sir, no older to that Boer child, I was to the harvest. The sea. Me and me da and me uncle in a small row boat wi' a glow of peat in the boat and a sail for covering of night. Fetchin' lobster out the water for five or six days at a go. On the water that length of time and me rowing the boat. For me Uncle was crippled in the back from a fall and me da, well, me da had not understood the English. We none of us spoke the English down there then, d'you follow me at all?'

Sullivan looked round the faces and they listened. It was still in the barn and not a man of them moved. Sullivan remembered when they brought his father home in the back of a donkey cart and there was talk that he would die. He had been only six and frightened as the women keened over this man, who had been crushed under the hooves of a horse.

'He'd stood in the way of some grand gentleman's horse and been ridden down for it, d'you see?' Sergeant Holly stirred.

'What's the point of this, Sullivan?'

Sullivan grinned. He knew he had touched a man at

108

last.

'It's a story only, Sergeant. I would only say that I think now I have seen both sides of the coin, sir.' He watched the officer to see how he was taking the story.

'I mean no disrespect, sir. Truly. But to be an Irishman, or worse, an Irishwoman, is to be kin to that lady in the farmhouse. Or the old lady who spat on you, sir.'

Richard did not move. He waited, stony-faced, for the man to go on. It was too late to stop him now and it might help him to understand this strange and difficult man if he heard the story.

'It is a business sir, to be truthful, that no man can wish on himself. We had at our door in Crookhaven a small patch of land for potatoes. It was our life, d'you see? Fish or potatoes. And in one year, the potatoes did not come. And the next. And people died, sir. And we did hear that further north they was shippin' grain from out of Ireland. That's the truth of it. And me ma and me da died. And there were empty cottages and bodies in the potato patch.'

The Sergeant was shouting something at him angrily and Sullivan could not hear anything now except the keening howl of the women, and he could see nothing but that black priest telling them it was the wrath of God for their sins. And him a child only.

'It is the same here, sir. We come to the land and we burn it. We are the pestilence now and I have heard the curses of our women at home and I'd not hear those curses on my head.'

He sat with his head bowed and did not look at them. For he felt sick in his stomach. He sat still and he heard only the birds screaming in the sky. He saw the soft water and the ruins of the cottages, with their roofs gone, and their walls the homes of dogs and wild cats and rats that fed on unmentionable offal.

The lieutenant had gone now and the men were lying down quietly to sleep. The sergeant was standing with the lamp looking at him. Sullivan stood and stared at the sergeant with no expression on his face.

'You're a bastard!' hissed the sergeant and blew out the lamp.

4

In the boy's room, Truus packed the small bag. He was awake and excited. In the leather bag was the boy's shirt, and some food. She also put a picture of his father and of herself and then from under her apron she took a pistol. She handed it to Piet.

'It is your father's gun,' she told him and he took it, checked it and smiled at her. She passed over some rounds of ammunition, which he pushed down into the bag.

'You will go now,' she said. 'When you can, tonight. Find the Wielver Commando. If any man stops you, tell him whose son you are. You will be safe.'

She knew Piet would be safe on the veldt. He was born to it. But she felt that she was wrenching away a limb, when she held him and kissed him.

'Please Piet, don't forget Rietsplaas. This is your place, your home. Whatever happens to it, to me, to your father, remember to come back to Rietsplaas. Promise me you will come back here.'

The boy was confused and didn't understand why his mother was making such a trouble of the matter. She was crying and he tried to stop her tears with his hands on her cheeks, but she took his hands and kissed them. She took the Bible and opened it at the front page and showed it to Piet. She gave him a piece of paper with names on it.

'These are your names, Piet. Your father and his father and his father before — I have written it down for you. Keep it.' He nodded.

'Now,' she said and stood up. 'When the time is right, go. Come back to Rietsplaas in a week, perhaps. Not sooner or they may catch you.'

'Shall I give my father a message from you?' he

asked and she shook her head.

Outside, a door slammed and Piet pushed the bag out of sight under the bedclothes. He got into bed and his mother kissed him again and held him for a moment. She let him go and walked to the door. There, she wiped her face and walked into the main room.

'Goodnight, Piet,' she said and closed his door.

In the room, Richard Gaunt sat at the table. He stood as she came in.

'Mevrou, d'you mind if I —' She shook her head. She didn't care. She walked to the door and looked out.

'An old lady spat on me today,' he said. 'I was stupid, I suppose. I found it a shocking thing.'

Truus didn't move. Outside, beyond the big trees, the stars shone in the black, clear sky.

'An old lady. She was quite alone. Very brave.'

Richard felt the uniform where she had spat. It was no longer damp, but he would remember it. Truus did not turn to look at him and he felt he was talking to stone. She did not seem concerned about him, about the soldiers, about anything. Somehow it was as if she was cut off from them all. As if she was many miles away.

Then he understood that, of course, she was many miles away — with her husband out in the dark land. Richard's mouth tightened. That man had been responsible for the deaths of Mallory and Clare, and a sergeant.

He stood up and walked over to the door and looked out. She moved away from him.

'It's fine land, Mevrou Meyer. At home, in England, I own land. Farms. Good farms too. Not the same as this farm. Farmed by tenants mostly. They're good farmers too.'

He would have given his right arm to be back in Gloucestershire now. There would be a frost on the long lawn and the hedges would be full of old man's beard, all rimed with frost,

I'm a fool, I suppose. But I do miss them, very much.'

She still would not look at him, but she did understand.

I'm sorry,' she said gently.

'Have I made a fool of myself?' he asked. Truus sighed and sat in her chair.

'Not at all. You are a young man.'

'I'm twenty-five.'

'My man was twenty-four when we married. He is a fine man.'

'The sooner this mess is finished, the better for us all, I think, Mevrou. The farm will need him.'

She shook her head and looked blindly at this fair-haired young soldier. He would never know the pain in her.

'I — I had news of him. Before you came.'

'Yes?'

'For a week, I have had pain. Here. Bad pain. Nagging at me. Bad pain. I know what it is now. He was shot on the veldt four days ago. I knew with the pain. I knew he was — he was shot by the English.' She looked again at Richard and he didn't know how to answer her. 'Have you ever *loved* anyone. Lieutenant?'

Richard stood silent on the veranda and shook his head. He had his orders and he had to obey them. She leaned back and shut her eyes. He looked down at the brown face and long, strong hands that were clenched in her lap. She began to rock in the chair and to keen softly.

Beyond the small pool of light from the lamp in the house, the veldt was black and still. Somewhere, a long way off, a dog howled, but otherwise the land was silent and the warmth that had been stored through the day rose into the night.

Truus opened her eyes and sighed.

113

'Your man brought the captain here?' Richard asked tentatively.

She said nothing. Her dark eyes stared. She did not even see him.

'The captain told me. I'm sorry.'

She leaned her head away from him, disappointed that the man should have betrayed her.

'I see.'

'Mevrou Meyer, it is very difficult for me. I have to — he is the leader of a Boer Commando.'

Truus looked down at her hands and then at this man who was tormenting her.

'He was shot. I told you.'

'But he was — you must understand, Mevrou Meyer, men were killed in the ambush at the river ten days ago.' She shut her eyes. 'Good men. Killed.'

'I understand you mister. And the captain was mended by me.' She leaned forward in her chair and her hands knotted the apron into a tight bundle in her lap.

'You want the killing to go on?' he asked.

'No. With all my heart. But I am powerless. When the war is taken to the women, I am sickened.'

Richard pressed home what he thought was his advantage.

'You help the rebels. So we are forced to bring the war to you.' She looked up at him and smiled a little.

'It makes you feel better to believe that.'

'We have orders, Mevrou.'

For a moment she looked fiercely at him and then she shut her eyes again. It was all over and she felt, somehow, slack in herself. Spent.

'I know you have orders. But please, should I refuse to help my own husband when he comes through? If you had a woman, would you expect her to turn her back? To make war against women is so easy. My man is now dead and my concern is not now with you. Send me to

114

detention camp, herd us together. It will make our men the more bitter. Gall in their souls. And you have your orders.' She was standing now and facing Richard.

'Mevrou, I have to do more than to take you to detention. I have to raze this farm to the ground.'

She looked at him and shook her head, uncomprehendingly. She did not believe him.

'You have land, Lieutenant? You told me you own farms. You would burn this place? Rietsplaas?'

'I am sorry, Mevrou.'

'I am sorry for you, mister. My man is dead and I have only Rietsplaas and you have your orders. Beg no blessing from me.' She sat down again in the chair.

He walked into her home. He lifted the latch of Saunders' door and walked in. Saunders was still reading his book. He glanced at Richard.

'You should have turned in, old man. Busy day tomorrow.' Richard stood looking down at the bandaged captain.

'You don't give a damn, do you?' Saunders sighed, closed his book with a thud and put it on the shelf over his head.

'No more I do, old boy. Listen, d'you think I give a farthing for that woman and her farm? It's nothing, Gaunt. I'd be coin, barter. She told me. Don't expect me to be grateful for that.'

Richard could feel the rough wall under his hand as he stood with his back to the wooden planks. Each hewn from the tree, each one fitted to the frame, each one worked by that man who was dead, somewhere on the veldt. Her husband, Boer leader, farmer, rebel. He was all these things and he had built this home for his wife and now Richard must burn it down. Surely Saunders could see the debt he owed that woman?

'You know Gaunt, you are a bloody prig. I'm glad to be alive. Might not have been. Chances of war, old boy.

115

'Doesn't mean to say I go about doing her favours.'

He despised Richard's weakness and he knew that he had to see to it that the decision was taken — and that Richard took it.

'You have an order. Burn if there is proof. I am the proof. What is there to hesitate over?'

'Truus Meyer.' Richard stood away from the wall and leaned on the rough hewn chair by the bed. Saunders shrugged.

'You'll take her back. She'll be sent down the line to detention camp.'

'Have you seen the detention camp?' Richard asked.

'Can't expect the Ritz, old boy. I didn't ask the Boer to fight.'

'Women, children herded together. Foul water, mud and tents. They die there, Rupert.' Rupert picked up his book and opened it.

'You're beginning to bore me, Richard,' he said.

Richard moved sharply over to the bedside. He was angry for the first time that Rupert Saunders had known him.

'You don't understand a thing, do you. Not a word gets through to that bland little mind of yours. No questions.'

'Orders, Gaunt. Captain Slingsby's orders. I understand you are not on good terms. Naturally I shall be putting in a full report. She's only one of thousands. What you do to her will make no difference — not to the war. But if you don't do it, well, you will be finished.'

'You'd threaten me, Rupert?' Richard was astonished even more than he was angry.

Saunders smiled blandly at him. Duty done.

'Would you order me, Captain?' Richard asked and Saunders, smiling still, shook his head.

'You're in charge here, old boy. Your show. Nothing to do with me. You make the decisions. I am merely the

116

proof. Ironic what?'

In the darkness, Jan Meyer's body was still being stripped of flesh. The black hat and the bandoleer lay where they had fallen, useful only to a man. Jan Meyer was a long way from Rietsplaas.

5

The sun was tipping the horizon beyond the trees at the edge of the field. The white and yellow light of the early morning. Soon, the animals would be stirring in the farm and soon, also, there would be water to raise from the well.

Truus looked blindly at the open Bible and tried to remember that she had no need any longer to concern herself with such things.

Richard watched the dawn light steal over the land. It would be hot today and dusty and he hated the thought of seeing Slingsby at the crossing, where the gun was. He wondered about the woman's husband. He'd be out in the veldt somewhere. Buried, he supposed. Such a waste of a good farmer.

Truus read aloud: "'May the sun come black as sackcloth of hair, and the moon as blood and the stars of heaven fall to earth . . .'" She looked up at him. 'The Lord does many things, Lieutenant. And says many things. I have tried very hard to understand why things happen as they do. You are a young man. War is surely for young men. Not for women too.'

She would not let him speak, then perhaps he would not say the words she dared not hear.

'Sometimes I wonder why we are here. Can I be here, so that you too can be here now?' She got up from the table and turned the Bible so that he could see it.

'My man wrote in the back here. The name of our child, Piet. See? It was Jan's father's book before that and another before — see? Names. Good people. Piet will have this book in his turn.' She sat at the table and began to cry.

He looked at the weeping woman.

'Mevrou Meyer, I have to obey my orders. You

118

know that.'

'We came in the early days. We came in wagons. Jan and I came to water and fine land and my man stopped and we have been here, on our land, since. Did your land come to you like that, through God?' She tossed her hair back to look at him through her tears as she asked the question. 'You cannot do this thing.'

'Sometimes people like you are hurt. I'm sorry.'

Truus was still now. The tears lay on her cheek. Outside, the sun rose and a bird crowed. The back room, where Piet had slept, was empty and the window was open to the morning light.

'Many of us didn't get this far,' she said.

Richard was helpless. Wouldn't she understand him? She had to go. To leave.

'I want you to get ready now.' She shook her head. 'We will burn this place down.' She wiped the tears from her cheek.

'I will stay.'

'There will be nowhere to stay.'

'Then I will have to build again.'

Richard was desperate. Outside, he could hear the men rousing themselves. Sergeant Holly had to be given his orders.

'Please, Mevrou. Have ready the things you can carry.' Truus looked about the room and indicated it with her hand.

'And this?' She looked at the books and the prints and the curtains and chairs and gleaming china and pots and pans and the pictures of herself and Jan on their marriage. He could not mean it. She could not accept it. She sat and laughed at him and pushed the long hair away again and refused to believe him.

'I'm sorry,' he said and she knew, now, that it had come to an end.

'Not really,' she said. 'Not truly. Are you?'

119

He looked down into her tired, drawn face and then turned and walked out quickly to the men. Sergeant Holly met him on the step and saluted.

'Morning, sir. Ready now sir?' Richard looked at him and, after a moment, he nodded.

'Let her take the things she can carry. No more.'

Holly shouted an order and five men from the section roared into the house. Richard stood outside and heard the rending of wood and the smashing of glass and china, the clatter of the pots and pans being flung about and the laughter of the men.

Sullivan stood on the step and watched him and when Richard saw him, the soldier walked away. Richard looked out at the buildings that were already being broken by the section. Two soldiers kicked and hacked at a water butt until it shattered and spewed water over the ground. Another kicked the chicken coop to pieces and yet another began a pile of straw and carts and wood near the main barn.

The sun was still low enough in the sky for the heat of the day to be only a promise. Holly came out of the house and across to Richard.

'Ready, sir. Give us the order, sir.'

Richard returned slowly to the room. Truus sat as she had been, when he left the room. Saunders was carried out of the ruins of the room.

It was a shambles. The men had enjoyed the destruction and had splintered fine chairs and ripped curtains and cushions. Feathers lay over the room like snow. Truus sat quiet and still and looked at him.

Holly came in behind him, with a lamp which was still alight.

'Couldn't find the little boy, sir. His window was open, sir,' he said.

'He is gone, Lieutenant. He is gone into the veldt. He will be a long way now and you cannot take him to any camp. He will fight you now, Lieutenant. Like his father did.' Richard said nothing.

Holly was impatient. 'Well, sir?'

Truus stared at him with her dark eyes that saw beyond him.

'Well?' she asked. 'Piet, he will remember Rietsplaas. He will remember. Go on, Lieutenant,' she said softly. 'Tell him. He wants to set it afire. Tell him. Tell him. Yes, he can obey an order. Yes.' She turned to Holly who was shocked by the madness on her.

'He will tell you. He will tell you.' She rose to face Richard, who wanted no more than to get out of here, to leave this sick and savage work and to let this woman alone.

'Have you your things, Mevrou? I did tell you.' She stood straight then.

'We had nothing when we came. A Bible only and a cart and a cow. Then I had a man, too.'

The men were standing awkwardly about the room, watching this woman as she spoke and as the tears ran freely now down her face.

'Look, they only want one word. Give them that word, Lieutenant. Give him that word. Tell the sergeant. When you give them that word to burn my place, I want you to remember. And when you are near the person you love, I want you to remember this place. Rietsplaas. Remember the flames and my man and my son who has gone. He fights only for this land -this place — he wants no more. Remember when you are near your woman and when she gets you a child. Remember.'

She knew as she looked into Richard's face that he would remember and she was sorry for him. She knew, also, that she had to help him to finish it all so she spat full in his face and he turned from her and gave the word.

'Sergeant Holly. Burn it.'

121

6

Nothing moved across the arid valley. The track to the crossing point of the Kaapshe river was dust and sharp stones. Beside the track, the scrub was thin and there were huge boulders standing above the arid earth.

The woman cursed them as they burned her home in Rietsplaas. And the flames rose in the still, early morning high above the veldt.

> Let their eyes be darkened that they see not
> And let their loins continually to shake.
> Let their habitations be desolate
> And let none dwell in their tents
> And let them not come into thy righteousness.
> Let them be blotted out of the book of the living.

And under the skull, white maggots moved softly in the rotten convolutions of the man's frontal lobes and the smell of war was low and foetid on the ground.

—ooOoo—